Heartache

The Twenty-Sided Sorceress: Book Five

Annie Bellet

If you want to be notified when Annie Bellet's next novel is
released and get free stories and occasional other goodies,
please sign up for her mailing list by going to:
http://tinyurl.com/anniebellet. Your email address will never
be shared and you can unsubscribe at any time.

Dedicated to all the authors that ever made me cry, and to Joss Whedon, the worst offender. I was angry, but now I think I understand what they felt.
Not that I have forgiven them.

The Twenty-Sided Sorceress
series in reading order:

The weather people had been forecasting a blizzard, but the sky was a smoky grey and the town utterly peaceful. Peace might have been nice if I didn't feel like the freaking sword of Damocles was playing hide and seek over my head. Alek was scarily full of a desire to keep me in his sights, which didn't help my anxiety levels one bit. I think he would have handcuffed himself to my side if I'd let him. My heart was forecasting doom.

Doom hadn't come. Nothing and nobody had come. Nearly a month had gone by since Samir's last missive to me. The dead apprentice of his, Tess, in my head was so damned sure he was coming for me, and yet…

Nobody came. The most eventful thing to happen was Brie's bakery being shut down for health code violations. As the building owner, I'd spent all Friday on the phone begging for a re-inspection and silently plotting revenge on the witches. Alek had cautioned that I should be sure they were responsible first. Voice of reason and all. It seemed likely someone had reported the magical cockroach invasion. The roaches were gone. Getting a re-inspection was a pain in the ass though. Neither Brie nor I could even remember the first one. The county bureaucrat might well have been a ninja.

I almost wished for ninjas. It would have given me something to fight against. Instead I spent four hours on hold and then got told to call back on Monday. Awesomesauce.

I wiped a dust cloth over a shelf that didn't have a speck of dust on it and wondered where Alek was today. He'd stuck next to me for weeks, hardly leaving my side, and then gone away an hour ago after getting a text message. When I'd asked him where the fire was, he had said only that he'd tell me later.

My door chimed and I turned toward the front of the shop, pulling on magic, almost hoping it was Alek so I could play the annoyed girlfriend. Him leaving like that, given everything going on, it made me even more nervous. I knew the chain around his neck was empty, though he tucked it beneath his shirt, but he'd only shaken his head and told me it was complicated when I asked. We'd come a long way down Trust Lane, but not all the way to Unconditional Trust-ville, I guess.

It wasn't Alek, but Brie who came through my door. Or, really, the triple goddesses who masqueraded as a single woman named Brie. She was tall and stacked, with bright red curls always braided up or piled on her head. Today her hair was neatly pinned back, her cheeks rosy from the chill air. She looked around my game store, peering into the corners, then, satisfied it was empty but for me, she gave me a half-wave and slumped into a chair.

"We're leaving," she said. "We've got to go, tonight. I was hoping you'd keep an eye on the building."

"What?" I pushed my hair out of my face as my guts twisted like rope inside me. "Leaving? For how long? You and Ciaran?"

"We've been called to Ireland," Brie said. Her eyes narrowed and she looked into a middle distance, staring toward the new release rack, but seeing something outside my understanding. She lapsed into Irish. "The fey are gathering. Ciaran must attend, and where he goes, so go I."

"What about Iollan?" I asked, thinking of the big druid. He and Ezee had seemed to reach a new level in their relationship. Like, having a relationship where they actually mentioned each other to their friends and family.

"Not he," Brie said, her eyes snapping to me as she shook off whatever thoughts had darkened her mood. "The druid cannot return to the Isle. But we must."

"So… you'll be back when?"

"I wish I could say."

The door chimed again and Ciaran entered in a sweep of crisp, icy air. The leprechaun wore his usual red coat and had a green army bag, like you'd see in old war movies, slung over one stout shoulder. His red and silver hair was tousled and damp, as though he'd showered and hadn't bothered to comb it.

"Brie tell you?" he said, also in Irish.

"She did, though I'm a little confused. Why now? Are you in trouble?" *Trouble I could fireball, perhaps?* I wanted to add, but made my will save. Or my Wisdom check? Either way.

Ciaran and Brie exchanged a look that didn't help my nerves at all. Then he shrugged one shoulder, the other probably weighted down too much by the rucksack to lift.

"We shall see," he said, lips pressing together at the end. "It has been five hundred years since the last gathering."

"Oh, well, maybe they miss your faces." I tried to smile. "Can I help? Are you magicking yourselves there or something?"

"We have a flight leaving from Seattle tonight. Max is driving us. He'll be walking in here through your back door in a moment." Brie rose, straightening her coat.

Max walked in through the back, setting my wards back there buzzing for a second.

Harper's brother grinned at me. "You really going to leave that door unlocked? Is that safe?"

"Anyone coming to kill me won't care about a ten

dollar lock on a door made of cardboard," I pointed out. "How's it feel to have your license, birthday boy?"

Max had turned sixteen the week before and the first thing he did was go get his license. Levi had gifted the kid a car that was ugly as sin and looked pieced together by a bad game of *Katamari* in a junkyard, but it ran despite being held together with bubblegum and love.

"Car's open if you want to put your stuff in," Max said as Brie and Ciaran both moved toward the back door. "I think they are in a hurry," he added to me as they disappeared down the back hall past the game room.

"Do I get to see the picture?" I resisted the urge to fluff Max's brown hair.

"Oh God, Harper told you?"

"Dude, really? Of course she told me."

"The camera went weird, I swear. I look like a cross-eyed chipmunk."

"Okay, it can't be that bad."

He shook his head and dragged his wallet out of his down jacket pocket.

It wasn't that bad. It was worse. I'm a terrible

person, but I totally laughed. There was no way *not* to laugh. I'm only human. Sort of.

Max yanked his license back and crammed it into his wallet muttering a bunch of words his mother would have washed his mouth out with soap for if she'd heard him.

"Hey, I'm sorry," I said, trying to stifle the giggles. "It's not so bad."

"Harper said the same thing. Then you know what she said?" Max's lips started to twitch and he was having trouble maintaining the surly teen boy act.

"What?"

"It's just, there's something about your eyes," he said in a high, squeaky voice that was supposed to be an imitation of his older sister. "Something... shifty." He switched back to his normal voice. "Seriously. Then she laughed so hard mom had to tell her to go outside."

"Did you tell her there is a special hell for people who make bad puns?"

Max rolled his eyes, then looked around us at the empty store. "Where is she, anyway?"

"Up at the college, in one of the library silent

ANNIE BELLET

study rooms. She's got MGL qualifiers to practice for and she says the net up there is better than here. Whole section of this block has turned into an annoying net deadzone. We drop offline all the time." I shrugged. The net was another annoyance, plus I missed Harper being here, cursing a blue storm. I felt weirdly lonely here in my store, just sitting around dusting things that were already clean and sorting cards already sorted.

Like someone rearranging deck chairs on the *Titanic*.

"Be careful on your drive," I said. I had enough intelligence to know not to question Max's car's ability to even make it to Seattle. His feelings were hurt enough for one day. "The roads and all. You going on to the beach early then?"

"Yeah, the guys got the house a couple days sooner than we thought." He and some friends had gotten a great deal on a beach house in Washington, it being winter and all. His sixteenth birthday was going a hell of a lot better than mine had.

I was glad he'd be away from Wylde for the week. If shit went down soon, one more person I cared about not in the crosshairs was good. Max had already gotten hurt because of me. I wished I could send them all away. But my friends had made their choice.

I could only hope it was the right one.

I made Ciaran and Brie promise to email me with updates, gave Max a quick hug, and stood in the freezing air to wave them away as Max's patchwork car bumped out of the parking lot and out onto the main road. I watched them disappear down the road and shivered from more than the winter chill. With that damned other shoe waiting to drop, every goodbye right now felt weirdly final.

My shop was so quiet and still when I returned that I almost missed Alek standing like a giant Viking shadow by the center support post. His white-blond hair was messy, the way it looked when he'd been running his hands through it, something he only did when upset or angry. His normally pale blue eyes looked colder than the sky and his mouth was pressed into a tight line.

"What's wrong?" I asked, feeling the metaphorical sword shoe thing lowering over my head.

"Carlos," he said.

"It's Sunday," I said, half to myself. The last few

weeks Carlos, Alek's friend and former mentor among the Justices, had been out of touch.

"He wants to meet. Wants me to meet someone."

"Where? When? Who?" I asked. I pressed my hands against his sides, wanting his heat, wanting to push back the tension and darkness lurking in his face and body.

"New Orleans. As soon as possible. I have no idea," he said. Then he shook his head. "No, I have an idea. I do not like it."

"Does he know about…" I looked at the chain disappearing under his collar.

"If I am to meet who I think, yes. He knows I am not a Justice anymore."

Alek's words hung between us, almost tangible, like fog in the air. So. There it was. Finally said.

"What happened, Alek?" I whispered. I had an idea. This, like so much else, was probably my fault. I tried to tell myself that was ego talking, but one couldn't deny the timing or the mounds of circumstantial evidence piling up around us.

"The world changes," he said. His eyes shifted down to my face and he bent, kissing me softly on the forehead. "This is not your fault."

He took a deep breath, his chest swelling big enough that his coat brushed my cheek. I wanted to lay my head against him and tell him everything would work out, but we were beyond lying to each other like that. I hoped.

"Anyway," he said after he let out the breath. "I am not going."

"What? Is this important? Will they try to hurt you?" I added the "try" because there was no way anybody was going to hurt him. Not on my watch.

"It is and no, I do not think they will. Carlos used our safe code. I do not think he would betray me, not like this. But it doesn't matter. I am not leaving you."

"So I'll come with you."

"You cannot travel where I would go."

"They have some kind of magical barrier around New Orleans now that keeps out sorceresses?" I tried to smile as I said it, ignoring the painful beating of my heart.

"It is Justice business. I am not sure even I can do what I must, but…" He sighed again. "I am not going."

Because of me. The tension in his body wasn't just

over worry about the situation. He wanted to go. Something had happened to him. One day he woke up and wasn't the same. The changes were tiny, things only I had noticed, I thought. The necklace being hidden. His over-attentiveness that went beyond worry about Samir. Every time he held me, he had a grip that made me feel like this would be the last time. He was here, almost stifling me, but somehow Alek seemed already gone.

If going, if sorting out this Justice business, would give a piece of him back, I couldn't let him stay. I wanted my Alek back, the man who was always sure of things, who saw the shadows in life and faced them down. Not this Alek who clung to me like the world was ending and I just couldn't see the explosion yet.

"You are going," I said.

"Jade," he started, but I shook my head.

"No. I'm serious. You haven't been you. I don't know what happened, because your stubborn ass won't tell me. But if going to see Carlos and whoever this other mysterious whatever is helps you come to terms with whatever the hell happened? I'm for it."

"I don't know how long I'll be gone," he said,

shaking his head slowly, his hair brushing against his cheeks and his expression torn between worry and desire. "What if Samir comes?"

"I've been asking myself that question for twenty-six years," I said as I forced my mouth to form a smile. It kind of hurt, but he needed me to be confident. "He hasn't shown up yet. We're about to get a pile of snow dumped on us. If you are going to leave, you should go. Take care of whatever you need to take care of. Then come home to me."

"I will always come home to you," he said and I swear to the Universe his eyes looked like he might cry.

The fuck was going on? I shivered again, despite the warm shop, despite his warm arms wrapping around me and pulling me close. Swords. Deck chairs. We were totally screwed—I just didn't know exactly how yet.

"Go," I said to him after he had kissed me hard enough that I wanted him to stay.

Alek pressed his cheek to mine and nodded slowly. When he left, I didn't say goodbye. I refused to, because this felt like goodbye enough.

All I knew was that if the Council of Nine did

anything to my lover, I was going to have to go make a whole new cadre of enemies. And if Alek didn't return to me soon, Carlos would be first on my damned list.

Sleeping alone that night, I dreamed of fire and ice. Snow and ash drifting down around me, burning my skin where it touched. Just after five in the morning, I gave on sleep and started a new play-through of *Skyrim*. The mindless task of leveling skills and crafting a few thousand iron daggers helped distract me, but I was still a bit of a zombie by the time I opened the shop.

"Jade?" Harper said. "Are you listening to me?"

I realized I'd been staring at the monitor not actually clicking the order button. A glance at the tiny clock in the bottom corner of the screen said it was noon. I wondered how long I'd been standing here, staring. My stomach clenched with hunger but my mouth tasted fuzzy and sour.

"Yeah?" I said, turning to her.

"You okay?" She peered at me with suspicious

green eyes, looking very inquisitive in a fox-like way that made me smile.

"Sure," I lied. "Just thinking about if I should order more custom minis. The last batch was pretty popular."

"Uh huh." Harper gave me a look that told me exactly what she was willing to pay for the bullshit I was trying to sell her. "I said the snow is starting to fall. I'm going to head up to the college to practice some seriously bad manner builds. If you don't need me," she added, worry creasing her forehead.

Fucking babysitters. I shook my head. "Nah, I'm good. What if it snows as hard as they say though?"

"Maybe I'll just hook up with a hot student and sleep over." She grinned.

I couldn't remember Harper ever dating anyone in the last five years, not anybody she'd introduced any of us to. I rolled my eyes at her. "Knock yourself out. But really?"

"Ezee gave me a key to his office. I can crash in the lounge on that floor. It's cool. They have popcorn and everything. Any other questions, mom?"

"Drive safe," I said, making a shooing motion.

She slung her bag over her shoulder but stopped short. "Are you sure you are okay here alone? I can't believe Alek left like that."

"Stop." I folded my arms across my chest. "First him, now you. Just quit, damnit. Nothing has happened in weeks. I almost wish it fucking would so we could stop walking around on eggshells waiting for sword shoes to fall on us. But Samir hasn't come at us directly, not once. I highly doubt he's going to start. Whatever happens, we'll have stupid amounts of warning. He's all about building terror and shit."

A funny warning bell went off in my head and a thought danced through my mind, as elusive as the snow starting to swirl in glittering flakes outside the store windows. I tried to grasp at it, but it melted away as Harper responded.

"Sword shoe?" Her brown eyebrows rose comically.

"Like waiting for the other shoe to drop. But also like the sword of Damocles, hanging by a freaking thread over me."

"You're weird," she said.

"Thanks, Captain Obvious. Now go, before it gets too snowy. I'll be fine."

"But what if Samir does show up?" she said, half turning toward the door.

"I'll challenge him to a wizard's duel. We'll play magical Rock-Paper-Scissors-Lizard-Spock."

"Like, super weird." Harper grinned. "But what if he sends another assassin?"

"I've taken on every bloody one he's sent. We're all here, they ain't. I think I can handle it. I mean, I've been training my ass off. Seriously, it's so flat I look Caucasian."

"Hey, I resemble that remark. Okay, fine. Just try not to have too much murderous fun without calling me first, deal?" Harper gave me a quick, tight hug, and finally left.

I smiled after her but felt the grin melt from my face as the shop grew silent again. I kind of didn't want to be alone, but everyone was gone. Levi at his shop, probably putting on his fiftieth set of snow tires and chains in the last week on some guy's car. Junebug and Rose at the Henhouse. Alek in NOLA. Ezee and Harper up at the college. Max on the coast. Brie and Ciaran on their way to Ireland.

Yep. Not creepy at all sitting in my shop alone waiting for sword shoes. Nope.

I texted Steve. Steve had Mondays off. I needed something to distract me and there was a new expansion of *Carcassonne* to test out. Steve had no idea about any of the weird shit. He wouldn't look at me sideways or be always looking over his shoulder, waiting for the next assassin or whatever Samir had planned now.

I called the county clerk again, trying to get another inspection. If I was going to be here alone, waiting for a random customer or for Steve to show, I figured I could make myself useful. Noon was lunch, apparently, and I got voice mail. I wanted to be able to tell Brie her bakery was open again by the time she returned. This whole mess was stupidly frustrating, and then for them to be called away in the middle? Super lame.

That formerly errant thought, which had been like snowflake and smoke before, crystallized.

Brie's shop shut down. Ciaran recalled to Ireland. Alek sent to New Orleans. The internet in town being spotty, forcing Harper away from the store more.

All these things leaving me here. Alone.

Another deep shiver went through me as I

clutched at my twenty-sided die talisman. Mind-Tess woke up, whispering a warning as Wolf, my spirit guardian, materialized, facing the door, growling.

I knew before I felt the wards hum. Before the door opened, bringing with it cold air, swirling snow, and the one man I had hoped never to see again.

I wasn't using Tess's magic, but time stood still anyway. My heart stopped. Blood froze in my veins. Samir walked two feet into my shop and stood, almost posed, the light glinting in his golden eyes, his long grey wool coat flaring with his sudden halt.

He was still handsome—his face all angles and evenly tanned skin, his hair black and artfully long over his forehead. Standing utterly still, feeling like a rabbit in the shadow of the hawk, I waited for my heart to reboot. I waited to see if I still felt. Still breathed. Mind-Tess fluttered nervously at the edges of my consciousness like a trapped sparrow.

Then time unfroze. Blood rushed to my head and

my heart slammed into my ribcage. I pulled my magic around me, reveling as strength and warmth poured through me.

I was no rabbit. Not anymore.

"So," I said, biting off the word with a murderous smile. "We meet again."

"Still funny, Jess. Or I suppose it is Jade, now." Samir smiled. Well, his lips shifted and curved upward, but nothing touched his eyes. They might as well have been molten gold in reality for all the emotion in them.

I wanted to blast him off his smug feet but held my rage in check, trembling with the effort of not unleashing hell on him. My wards were humming and I smelled the honey scent of his power. He wouldn't have walked in here without some kind of protection. Hell, he hadn't even looked at Wolf where she crouched growling, her long tail swishing like a cat's. Either he couldn't see her, or…

He wasn't worried. The tiny part of my brain that wasn't insane with hatred told me that should worry *me*.

I unclenched my fists and wrapped my left hand around my talisman, fighting for control of my emotions, of my power.

"It's always been Jade," I said. I sent a tendril of power at him, probing the air around him, ready with a shield if he reacted.

Samir kept smiling. My magic slid off an invisible barrier a few inches out from his body. He was shielding. Damn.

What had I expected? It was never going to be as easy as magically punching my way into his ribcage and ripping out his bleeding, shriveled heart.

"Twenty-six years, and you just walk into my store?" I said. I pulled my magic back, thinking furiously about how to get through his shield. Bring the building down on him? Nobody but me was here. I discarded the idea even as it formed. It would probably just piss him off.

"Things around here have gotten too interesting to resist." He shrugged, never taking that molten gaze off me.

"You mean you finally decided to man up and come after me yourself?"

"Man...up?" Samir grinned and took a step forward, reaching a hand out as though he wanted to brush my cheek with it.

I swelled with magic, purple sparks crackling in the air around me. Maybe bringing down the building wouldn't be the worst idea. Not compared to if he touched me. My skin wanted to crawl off and burn itself alive at the suggestion of his hands on my body again.

"You truly think I was working up the courage to face you, child?" He laughed, but he didn't advance further. "I hate to bruise your ego, my dear, but I have other pursuits in life."

"Yeah fucking right," I said through gritted teeth. "You've hunted me for years. And now that you've found me again, you just. Won't. Leave. Me. Alone." I bit off every word, spitting them out, my whole body trembling with the effort not to smash him down. My rage scared me a little, scared mind-Tess, too, who had gone silent.

The only one not scared was Samir. He was laughing again, his head thrown back, his eyes finally off me.

I took my chance. The floor in here was concrete under the thin, industrial carpet. I slammed my magic down into it, sending a wide crack at Samir. His shield might turn my magic, but I wanted to see how he felt about being sunk into concrete that turned instantly to quicksand beneath his feet.

Samir sprang back and a wave of magic radiated off him, smashing into my own shield and sliding me backward as though I'd been physically shoved. My tailbone jammed into the counter behind me and I heard glass crack. I hoped it was glass, anyway, and not my bones. Pain barely registered, hot but distant, like standing just within the circle of warmth from a bonfire.

The walls groaned, but the building stood. I'd sunk a lot of warding magic into it. A crack and a missing couple feet of flooring wouldn't bring it down.

I'd have to do better. I circled to my right, away from the counter. Wolf circled with me, her lips in a silent snarl.

"I've known where you were for four years, Jade," Samir said.

"Bullshit," I said, but his words were like another blow and I stopped moving, watching him, ready for another spell if one came. "If that's true, why not come after me four years ago?"

"Why rush? You would have run again. Chasing

you around was interesting for a few years, but then it became routine. And I do hate routine. Ask Tess." His smile was back, but less confident than before. "Ah yes, you can't. Poor Tess."

In my mind, the ghost of Tess, her soul, or whatever the hell she was now, agreed with him. Boredom was Samir's true enemy. She assured me that she had known nothing about him being aware the whole time of where I was. Small comfort. I hoped he was lying. Alek could have told me, but Alek was away. Which was good. My love would have just gotten himself killed in minutes trying to defend me.

"Here you stayed, surrounded by your childish games. Quiet and boring as a mouse, scratching away at life. Sad, broken, terrified of shadows. Already broken toys hold no interest for me."

I studied his face, an odd grief tempering my rage. I had loved him, once. But it was so clear now, more clear than ever, pushed home by years and by my new experience of actual love, that what I had felt for Samir had been as immature and naïve as I once was. And the Samir I had loved so blindly had never been real.

I clung to the rage, shoving away all other feelings. This was not epiphany time. This was supposed to be ass-kicking time.

Him monologuing was good though. It always killed villains in movies. I tried to keep him talking.

"Why not just fuck off and stay away then?"

"You got interesting. My little mage. Taking her first heart. Thrilling, isn't it? Gaining power, soaking in the knowledge of another, absorbing their spark into your own growing light until you are the sun and moon and stars."

"Have you spent the last few decades smoking crack? I wish you'd said shit like that when I first met you. I probably would have smothered you in your sleep just to shut you up." I circled more to the right. About seven more steps and I would reach the door.

Not that I should take the fight outside, but I had a dim thought of leading him away from town. This was Wylde; there were woods within a quick run from anywhere, including my store. Out in the open, away from humans and buildings, we could get our wizard dueling on.

"Would anything convince you I am not a monster?" His smile faded, his expression turning to stone.

"Hmm. Sending assassins after me. Fucking up my birth family and getting my father killed. Oh yeah, that part where you fucking burned everyone I ever loved to death. So. That's a big ass cup of nope." I willed Wolf to make for the door, trying to telepathically send her the plan. Maybe she could help cover my retreat. She'd hurt him before. It was worth a shot.

"Then there is no use pretending. You know what I want."

"Why did you send the postcard? If you thought I'd run," I added as he raised an eyebrow.

"To see if you would. And when you didn't, I knew that you had grown roots again. I knew that you had something to lose again."

His words worked like a *Petrification* spell.

"So you have been fucking with us." It wasn't a question. All the pieces I'd put together too slowly were locking into place. "Why not just kill me?"

Samir shook his head and started to answer, but the chime of my door interrupted him. In my peripheral vision, I saw Steve's head appear, followed by his wide shoulders wrapped up in a green parka.

Snow was melting on his chubby, cheerful cheeks. He was smiling as he stomped his feet on the doormat and raised one hand in greeting as he tugged off his ugly Christmas scarf with his other.

"Steve," I screamed at him, "get out!"

Steve's eyes went wide and his mouth opened as though to ask a question. The words were cut off by a gossamer thread as it flew through the air from Samir and wrapped around Steve's exposed throat. Blood sprayed in fine mist and Steve collapsed to his knees, his hands going to his neck.

I slammed a wave of power at Samir, shoving him back, and sprang for Steve. My fingers felt stiff and numb as I tried to get to the magic garrote cutting its way into Steve's neck. The thread felt like fishing line, slippery with blood and gore. Steve convulsed and choked, blood gushing out of his mouth and air starting to hiss from his cut throat.

Blood, blood everywhere.

"Tess," I cried, not caring that I was talking aloud. I reached for mind-Tess, begging her to help me fix this. She was the caged bird again in my head, her ghost screaming at me to stop trying to save a dead man and pay attention to the enemy coming at me.

I reached for her memories, but there was no time to sift, to learn. No time.

Time. I could do things with time. Things I was learning from Tess.

NO. Mind-Tess still screaming.

I twisted my magic from defensive shielding and poured my will into it, the desire formed by my need, the thought of what I wanted not even registering at a wholly conscious level.

I wanted Steve to be not dying. I wanted time to save him.

Magic roared in my ears, drowning out the voice in my head, the sound of Steve choking to death on his own blood only inches from my face. I wrapped a bloody hand around my talisman and threw my power into action.

Time. I needed more time.

The world faded in a purple spiral, my whole body seizing as magic pooled around me, drowning me. I felt like I'd jumped in a wormhole, all sensation fading as I plummeted into a whirlpool of noise and sensation. I squeezed my eyes shut, hoping I still had eyes. There was noise like rushing water or heavy wind or the beating of a million angry wings.

And then it stopped and the world was quiet. I opened my eyes, staggering as my legs threatened to drop me onto my ass.

I was in my store. No Steve. No blood on my hands. Wolf leaned into me, holding me up as I stumbled forward, toward the door. Samir was talking, saying something about not being ready. I realized I'd let go of my power. I wasn't even shielding. My evil ex was too busy with the sound of his voice to notice yet.

He stopped talking and narrowed his eyes. I reached for my power again and was answered with only a thin sputtering trickle, like when the water has been shut off but you still get what's left in the pipes.

What the fuck had I done? Where was Steve? The shop walls were pushing in on me, my head pounding as though I'd slammed it into the wall a few dozen times.

Samir shook his head and started to say something else, but the chime of my door interrupted him. In my peripheral vision, I saw Steve's head appear, followed by his wide shoulders wrapped up in a green parka. Snow was melting on his chubby, cheerful cheeks. He was smiling as he stamped his feet on the doormat and raised one hand in greeting as he tugged off his ugly Christmas scarf with his other.

Déjà-fucking-vu.

"Steve," I screamed at him, "get out!"

I knew that Samir would throw the killing magic. I watched it almost in slow motion as it swished through the air, a silvery thread of death.

Springing straight into its path, I felt an odd cold pain in my neck as the thread hit me, and then passed right through as though made of nothing more than imagination and smoke.

I tried to cast a spell, to throw up a shield, anything, but magic failed me, flowing out of my veins like sand in a sieve. I grabbed for Steve as he fell, as blood misted from his throat.

Once it hit him, the thread became tangible. I jammed my fingers into it and tried to pull it away from his throat. Cold fire burned into my joints, my skin recoiling from the magic.

"No," I said, over and over. "No, don't you die on me again. No. Steve."

Steve tried to say something, but it came out as an aspirated gush of blood. His eyes bulged.

Then he died in my arms, my fingers numb and clinging to the magic that killed him, buried in his throat.

Only hatred kept me conscious. My eyes were wet with unshed tears, my vision fogging as Samir walked toward me. Wolf snarled and tried to spring at him, but hit his shield in a spray of black smoke and disappeared, materializing again three feet beyond him, still snarling.

"Why?" I asked, my voice raw and unable to rise above a stage whisper. My throat felt as though it had collapsed on itself and my hand slipped from the garrote as trembling took over. My body refused to obey me and I crumpled, half-sitting on Steve's still chest. Broken.

"Give me Clyde's heart," Samir said.

"Why did you do this? He's just a guy."

"Clyde's heart, where is it? Perhaps I will spare the next guy, hmm?" Samir's cold smile was back.

I wanted to kick his teeth in, but I wasn't sure I even had feet. I couldn't feel them anyway.

"I don't have it," I started to say, but decided not to. He wouldn't believe me. "Just end me," I whispered instead. I couldn't defend myself.

Whatever I had done, turning back time like that, it had wiped the floor with me.

I'd defeated myself.

"Kill you? Here? Like this? Oh, Jade. You do not understand, do you? This ws just a warning. Give me the heart, and spare us both this drama." He smiled down at me with a shake of his head.

"Why won't you?" I screamed. My voice gave out mid cry. "Please," I added, the word forming on my lips but no sound carrying it out into the room.

"Because, my dear," Samir said. "I'm not bored yet."

He left my shop, his shape a shadow as he disappeared into the swirling snow.

I swallowed tears and nausea, adrenaline draining away as quickly as my magic had. I forced myself to look down at Steve.

"I'm so sorry," I mouthed to him.

He didn't answer. He'd never answer.

Working slowly, my stiff hands and the vast amount of blood causing me to lose my grip constantly, I tugged the garrote from his neck. It was inert now, appearing very much like fishing line. Thin and clear. Like my grief, like the tears running down my cheeks and spilling onto my collarbones.

That's how the deputy from the sherriff's office found me. Kneeling over Steve's corpse, garrote in my bloody hands.

They told me I had the right to remain silent, but it didn't matter. I had no voice and nothing at all to say.

3

Snow fell in whirling curtains, the chains on the tires rattling like ghosts as the deputies drove me down the road to the county station. I felt the air on my skin as the bigger deputy, a bearded man whose name I wouldn't have been able to remember on a good day, pulled me out of the back, but my legs wouldn't hold me up. All I saw was Steve's dead face and his eyes clouding over.

I threw up on the stairs and there was nothing in my stomach but yellow bile. They hauled me into the station, still dry heaving. Heat hit me as we stumbled through the double doors.

Maybe Tess was right. Maybe there was a hell and

these were the gates. I choked on more bile and tried to speak, but my throat was still ruined, my jaw like nails and broken glass. I needed my phone call. I had to warn Harper. I had to warn them all. I tried to make my eyes focus, to make Steve's face stop swimming in front of me. *Wolf. Tell Harper that Timmy fell down the well again.* I mentally reached for her but even thinking hurt. I couldn't see her anywhere. I couldn't call out.

No voice. No guardian. I was alone here. Helpless. Just heat now, and the scuffed hardwood floor rising to meet my face like a punch I totally deserved.

"You left her cuffed?" A woman's voice was arguing with a man's. Sherriff Lee. "I can't believe you just left her unconscious like that. Where's the damn doctor? Did you even think to call a paramedic? She's covered in blood."

"It's not hers, we checked," a defensive male voice responded.

Hands touched me and I tried to unglue my

eyelids. Metal clinked on metal as Lee removed my cuffs. I opened my eyes and met her light brown gaze. My shoulders unkinked as I pulled my hands in front of me, blood rushing back into my fingers with the vengeance of a thousand needles.

Blood. On my hands. Steve's blood. It had dried to a sticky brown color, as though I'd been holding onto something rusted. Broken. Steve. Shit.

"Jade?" Lee said softly.

I dragged my gaze away from my hands and sat all the way up. I was in one of the four holding cells in the back of the county courthouse. Such as it was, anyway. The courthouse was tiny, a converted church that had been added onto for the last century. Two court rooms, one for traffic, one for everything else. Four cells. The sherriff's office and a bull pen for the handful of deputies. Offices upstairs for the presiding judges, all two of them. Anything serious went up to the state facilities—not that most stuff that happened in Wylde was ever written up. Lee and her shifter deputies kept things quiet and swept the weird shit under the proverbial rug.

I worked my jaw, wincing. I didn't know how long I'd been out, but my magic was there when I reached for it. The stream was thin and weak, but at least I could keep hold of it without vomiting or passing out. I reluctantly let it go and tried out my words. I felt the warm weight of my D20 talisman against my chest beneath my shirt. They hadn't taken that, at least.

"I need to call Harper," I said. My voice was mostly back, thick with grief and pain, but audible at least.

"She's awake? Sherriff, you can't be in there," another male voice, different from the earlier one, called out. Heavy footsteps rounded the corner and a man who was nearly as wide as he was tall, which wasn't much taller than I, charged down the hall toward my cell. He looked about forty with thinning hair he'd tried to comb over and a suit that had probably been wrinkled before it was crammed into a winter coat. He had a badge clipped to his belt, but no gun, just the worn spot on his belt where one would clip on.

"She needs to get checked out by a paramedic," Lee said, straightening up. Very quickly and so softly I wasn't sure I even heard her, she added, "I already called her. You have a lawyer?"

"Call her again. Tell Harper that Samir is here. Tell her to turtle." Harper would know what I meant. We'd been thinking, planning what would happen if or when Samir showed.

"Lee," the angry man said. "You want this in your report too? One would think you have enough troubles right now."

"She's our suspect," said another man, coming up behind the other. He was the Jack Sprat to Angry Man's rotundity. In his thirties, with sandy hair and bland blue eyes, he wore a button down shirt with no jacket. He too had a badge but no gun.

"I didn't do it," I said. Partially because I was probably expected to, and partially for Lee. She had to know I didn't do this. She had to believe me.

"Jade, these are detectives with the State Police," she started to say, but Angry Man pushed past her and grabbed my arm.

I almost hit him in the face with my palm like Alek had been teaching me to do, but figured I shouldn't add assault to my growing record. So I shook his hand off, giving him my best "I will fucking murder you" look instead. I'd learned that from Alek also. He had a very convincing murder face.

"Come with us," he said.

Apparently I was a good student, because Angry Man backed off and let me stumble out of the cell on my own. They led me out into the bull pen. It was empty but for Jack Sprat, who preceded us. From there I was taken to the interview room, which was about ten degrees colder than the rest of the building.

I knew from cop shows that this was to make me uncomfortable, but the cool air felt good on my feverish skin. All I needed was a drink of water, ten hours in a shower scrubbing myself down with sand, and I'd feel almost normal again.

Oh, and for Samir to be dead and Steve to be alive. That too.

I folded my arms on the metal table and put my head down, closing my eyes against the glare of the fluorescent lighting. I'd rested a little, but I was far from strong. Miles and acres and lightyears and parsecs away from being strong enough. My body felt hollow, like a bell that had been rung too many times and now was left with the semblance of vibration and noise.

"Your name is Jade Crow?" Angry Man asked.

"Lawyer," I said. Fuck these guys. I had such worse problems, they didn't even know.

"You are being charged with first degree murder," Jack Sprat said. "Why don't you tell us your side. Did that man try to hurt you?"

He probably thought he sounded genuine. He sounded like an asshole.

"Steve," I said, baited into raising my head up and talking. "His name is Steve."

"Was Steve," Angry Man said. His thick lips were pressed into a wormy line in his pallid face and I started to wish I'd hit him.

"Why did you kill Steve?" Jack Sprat asked.

"I didn't," I said. "Lawyer."

"If you aren't guilty, why do you need a lawyer?" Jack was losing his patience.

I stayed silent and looked down at the table. My hands were the only thing covered in blood. I stank of it—my jeans, my shirt, everything was spattered and soaked. I resisted looking across into the two-way glass, not wanting to see myself. I probably looked like a Native American version of *Carrie*. Though my mouth tasted like shit and ass, I didn't want water anymore. I'd just throw it up.

"Look, you'd better talk to us. You know they still have the death penalty in Idaho, right?"

"You want to spend the next decade rotting in the Pocatello Women's Correctional Center?" Jack Sprat added.

"I thought you were supposed to be good cop," I said, baring my teeth at him.

The younger detective started to say something but a quick hand motion from his partner stopped him. Angry Man, now looking more comically sly than angry, approached the table and sat down across from me.

"Look, Jade, we're trying to help you. That crime scene, well, it was ugly. But we do just want to understand. Let's get off on a better foot here, all right?"

"Wait, so now you are good cop? I'm so confused." I folded my hands, trying to obscure the worst of the blood. I just wanted to stop thinking about blood. About Steve's blood. My stomach twisted and I swallowed hard to keep the acid down.

"I'm Detective Dickson and this is my partner, Detective Baldwin," Angry Man said.

I tried to choke back a laugh and failed, snorting painfully through my nose. "Wait, so you're telling me that you guys are Dick and Balls?"

"You fucking crazy bitch," Balls growled, coming at me.

Dick could move, I'd give him that. He got between his partner and I and ordered the younger man to go get me a soda.

"Dick and Balls. That's funny," he said, his face tight and his eyes mean in a way that said he was lying through his teeth but still trying for the good cop role. Definitely wasn't going to get callbacks for that part.

"What? You guys have never heard that one before? Seriously?" It seemed stupidly obvious and cops liked nicknames. At least TV cops did.

"There's a blizzard outside, Jade. We just want to get home to our families. So why don't you go over your version of events and you can have a shower and get some sleep."

"L. A. W. Y. E. R," I said, spelling it out for him. Then I put my head back down and closed my eyes again.

Balls came back with a cup of coffee which I

didn't touch. The acidic, stale smell alone made me more nauseated. I kept my head down and my eyes closed, ignoring their various questions until they finally left the room after Dick cuffed my right hand to a ring in the table.

Samir was out there. He wanted Clyde's heart. So he'd said.

"A diversion," Tess whispered in my head.

I was inclined to agree. Oh, I was sure Samir did want the heart. Somehow he knew I hadn't eaten it. Maybe because of the bag. It was Samir's creation, after all, so he might know when something was inside it. I'd given the bag to Alek to hide, so I wouldn't be tempted by the power in it. I wanted no part of that evil.

Which, I admit, was looking stupid and squeamish of me now. Samir had been toying with me. Wiping my own floor with me, if I was honest. I didn't want to be honest. I wanted to commit some serious murderating for real.

So why Clyde's heart? Why kill Steve? What was Samir going to do next and how the hell did I get out of this stupid place and find him?

And what the fuck had I done in my shop?

"You went back in time," mind-Tess said. With my eyes closed, I could see her, the beautiful ghost in my head sitting on a rock inside a silver circle. "That shouldn't have worked."

"It sure fucked me up," I muttered, remembering the weakness, the sputtering and utter failure of my powers.

I reached for my magic again and the tap turned on. More of a bathroom sink kind of tap than the firehose I was used to, but better than before. Maybe enough that I could bust myself out of this joint. There was no clock. I could have been unconscious for minutes or for hours.

Samir knew I had something, or more importantly, someone, more than one someone, to lose now. Again. And he had who knew how much of a head start on hurting them.

Fuck the law. I wasn't staying in here. Gripping my D20 in my left hand, I channeled my magic down my right arm and threaded it around the handcuff.

Wolf appeared beside me and whined, pressing her head against my side. My magic stuttered and halted, fading from my control.

"The fuck you doing?" I whispered to her.

Voices from the bullpen drew my attention just as the door slammed open. A petite woman with wheat-blond hair and bright blue eyes sailed into the room, carrying a briefcase and the air of command. She pulled a chair away from the wall, set her briefcase on the table, and then kicked the door shut with her heel.

I relaxed slightly. Maybe I wouldn't have to add running from the law to my résumé just yet. The cavalry had arrived.

Kate Perkins, Esquire, was as much a bomb as she was bombshell. She was joint partner in the only law firm in town, Perkins & Smitt. Harper liked to call them Perky and Smitten, which was apt enough since an astronaut could have seen the giant torch Harrison Smitt was carrying for the beautiful blonde. Kate's real name was Katya Gararin and Harper had told me she was a cougar shifter who had come over from the Ukraine with her family, fleeing the Iron Curtain.

I'd met Kate about three years before when she needed documents translated. She'd tracked me down after one of the shifters who owned the RV park outside town, Mikhail, had told her I was fluent and did translation work. I was certified to do work for the court in six different languages, though not all of them under my own name. She'd been a breeze to work for, paid on time, and didn't ask questions.

Since then, I'd been doing odd translation jobs for her when she needed, but I was still surprised she had shown up here. She didn't do criminal law that I knew of beyond the occasional DUI or pot-smoking bust.

"Are you hurt?" Kate said, looking me over.

"Not physically," I muttered. "Are you my lawyer?"

"The Macnulty girl called me. I called Sheriff Lee, who said you'd been arrested for murder. Can we do this in Russian?" she added, switching to Russian with an exaggerated look at the two-way mirror.

"Don't trust Dick and Balls to keep client confidentiality sacred?" I glanced at the mirror also and wished I hadn't. I looked worse than a horror movie in the dark glass. A wraith. A nightmare.

"Dick and…" she trailed off and laughed. "Dickson and Baldwin. Nice one."

"I didn't do it," I said in Russian, unable to share

her mirth. "The man who did is out there, and he'll do this again."

"I know you didn't do it," Kate said, her own face turning serious in a blink. "I saw the crime scene photos and talked to the coroner."

"Assuring yourself of my innocence before you took me as a client?"

"Yes. I was. I like you, and I owe Alek, but I don't need a first degree murder case." She sat back in her chair and watched me.

After a long moment she continued, "As soon as those idiots get their evidence in order, they will also realize it's impossible you did this. I'm going to make them clean you up, and then we'll answer some of their questions. Did you say anything to them yet?"

"Other than calling them Dick and Balls?" I said. "Nope. I can't exactly tell them the full truth. I'd just end up in a straight jacket."

"You are lucky I owe Alek," she said, but her mouth twitched in a half smile.

Kate left and came back with a Styrofoam cup of water and a warm washcloth. She glared at Dick until he undid my cuff and they let me wipe off my hands. I resisted quoting Shakespeare, since Lady

Macbeth had actually been a killer and I didn't really want to draw unnecessary parallels. But I was freakishly glad to have at least some of the blood off my hands.

"My client is willing to answer some questions," Kate said, after looking at me to see if I was ready.

There were only three chairs in the room, so Balls was forced to stand awkwardly against the wall as Dick sat across from us, placing a brown folder on the table.

"Will she answer why she killed Steven Jones?"

"If this is your line, we're done," Kate said, starting to rise from her chair.

"She was kneeling over the body, with the murder weapon in her hands. We have a damned deputy as witness, not to mention whoever called nine-one-one." Dick shook his head.

Someone had called nine-one-one? That explained how quickly the deputy had found me. But no one had been around.

"Male or female?" I asked.

"What?" Balls and Dick both squinted at me.

"The caller. Male or female?"

Dick pulled open the file folder and skimmed

down what looked like a report sheet. I wondered again how long I'd been out. Long enough for crime scene photos and Kate to check with the coroner. I looked down at my hands again and then at the bloody rag.

"Um, did I just destroy evidence?"

Dick and Balls exchanged another look, this one more worried.

"Nobody examined you? Did they are least take pictures?"

"I was kind of unconscious," I said.

"She was out cold. Besides, witness. I told you already."

"Did you process her in at all?" Kate gave the detectives a flat look that said she was super unimpressed.

"She's been charged with murder. The DA will make it official in front of the judge tomorrow. If he can get here with all the damned snow." Dick tapped the folder. "It's all here."

"Did you look at the coroner's report?" Kate spoke like she was dealing with children, each word carefully enunciated.

"Yes." Nods from both men.

"How much did Mr. Jones weigh?"

"A couple hundred, I guess."

"Two-hundred-thirty-seven pounds. How much does my client weigh?"

"I've always been taught you don't ask a lady her age or her weight," Dick shot back with an angry smile. The meanness was back in his eyes, but beads of sweat popped out on his forehead like dew.

"One-thirty," I said. I saw where she was going with it, and relief snaked through me. I was about to be exonerated through science. The irony was not lost on me.

"So, this girl took down a man who outweighed her by over one hundred pounds, without defensive marks or bruising on either of them, then used a length of what appears to be guitar string to half sever the victim's head, again without leaving a cut or bruise on herself. Not a mark on her hands. Nothing."

I obediently held my hands up, palms out. Tried really hard not to hear her words and think about Steve's throat gaping. About his dead eyes. I failed and had to turn aside, dry-heaving again. I put my head between my knees to fight the dizziness, but it was a mistake. My pants were coated with blood and all I could smell was sickness and death.

Kate gently patted my back and made me drink some of the water. I tried to tell her it would just end up on her expensive shoes, but she waved that off.

Both detectives were quiet for a good minute, chewing over what Kate had just pointed out. I probably had sexism on my side on this one, since it was pretty obvious from their expressions that they had no trouble doubting a skinny chick like me with my non-existent nerd muscles had taken out a big grown man like Steve.

"That's for the DA to decide. She's been arrested. Now, if she has an alternate story she wants to tell, we're listening," Dickson said finally.

"It's okay," I said, looking at Kate. "I'll tell them exactly what happened."

Except, of course, for the parts that would bring the men in lab coats.

So I couldn't tell them the whole truth. I skimmed all the magic parts and waved off a question about the giant crack in the floor from Baldwin. But I gave them the gist. Killer psycho ex-lover out to hurt me, who came to my shop and attacked my friend.

"Describe this guy for us?" Dickson actually had a pen out. He glared at Baldwin when the younger detective snorted and shook his head.

"About six foot one. Black hair a little longer than Balls' over there. Gold eyes, they look like contacts but they aren't. Skin a shade or so lighter than mine, less brown, more just tanned looking. He was wearing a grey wool coat." *And will probably kill you if you get too close or try to detain him*, I added silently. "He's very dangerous," I said instead. I hoped that Samir would at least be trying to fly below the human world's radar. He'd never drawn huge attention to himself that I knew of, at any rate. Maybe a little law pressure would get him to back down, give me space to come up with a new plan.

I was grasping at desperate straws, I knew, but they were all I had.

"So this guy came in, killed Steven, and then just walked away? Why was the wire in your hands?" Dickson had his good cop face back on though it was even less convincing than before.

I waited a beat for Kate to say I didn't have to answer that, but I guess she was too busy lawyering to watch the amount of crime shows I had. Instead she looked at me and raised a perfectly waxed eyebrow.

"I was pulling it out. Trying to help him. He died in my fucking arms and I couldn't do anything." I bit down on the inside of my cheek, tasting blood, trying to focus on anger instead of grief. Instead of my failure. "I couldn't do anything," I whispered, looking away from everyone, my eyes focused on a paint chip on the blank beige wall.

"I think that is enough for you to get started, detectives," Kate said firmly. "My client is exhausted and I'm sure she would like to go home."

"She can't go home," Balls said. "She's under arrest."

"Did you not hear a thing I've said?" Kate pursed her lips, her gaze turning to ice.

"That's for the DA to decide, and the judge. Not us. We made the arrest, we can't just let her walk. She's got to appear tomorrow." Dick ran a hand through his thinning hair, completely screwing up his comb-over.

"I can't stay here," I said to Kate. "He's out there. Who knows what he's doing to my friends."

"It's snowing so hard you can't see your shoes. Nobody is gonna be killing anybody tonight, if this guy even exists." Balls gave a disgusted snort.

There was more arguing back and forth, but my head started to pound again and I put it down on the table. The metal felt cold and soothing against my skin. It was clear that Kate had planted doubt in the detectives' minds, but they wouldn't budge on letting me go. It seemed like they'd hustled their asses down here for the sure collar, but now that things were messier than a girl covered in blood writing up a tidy confession, they wanted to pass that buck off to someone else.

Me? I just wanted to murder someone for real. Or sleep. I missed Alek. He'd rip right through these walls, stare down these assholes, and get me out. At least, my tired brain had that fantasy. I knew the reality would be different. Besides, part of me was glad he was gone. At least in NOLA he was safe from Samir.

Unless somehow Samir had tricked him into going there. I sat up, grasping at that thought, worried more than ever.

"I want my phone call," I said.

"Cell tower is out. Landline is screwed, too. Won't do you any good. Sorry," Balls said in a way that made it clear he wasn't sorry at all.

So that was it then. I was stuck in jail for the night while my friends were out there in a frakking blizzard, with my psycho ex stalking them. I tried to tell myself they were capable, smart people who knew the danger, but it was cold comfort.

Kate walked me back to the bathroom as the deputy on duty went hunting through the lockers to find me some sweats and a clean shirt. They made her stay in the room with me while I showered, not that I could have fit through the tiny window anyway. What was I going to do? Charge off naked into a blizzard?

I ignored that I had been about to do something very close to that before Kate showed up, and scrubbed my skin raw. Barely able to stay on my feet but glad for warm clothes and no more blood matting my hair, I stumbled back to my cell and sank down on the thin mattress.

"First thing tomorrow, I'm going to get you out of here. Even if I have to put Ray into a snowplow and drive him here, all right?" Kate smiled at me. I assumed Ray was the district attorney. Or maybe the Judge. I wasn't exactly on a first name basis with either.

"No," I said, trying not to sound ungrateful but feeling surly and exhausted—and scared. "It isn't all right. But what choice do I have?"

"Get some sleep. It's late. You'll barely even notice the night going by. I'll be back soon. Trust me, okay? I'm your lawyer." Kate smiled, patted my shoulder gently, and then left.

Dick and Balls must have left, too, because nobody disturbed me. I heard the deputy on duty out there listening to soft Jazz, but he left me alone. The lights were dim, only the one in the hallway on and its glow didn't quite reach the bed. I pulled the blanket over myself and lay back, my thoughts charging in crazy circles around my brain. Finally I reached for my magic and wove a simple ward around the cell, anchoring it to the corners. It wouldn't do much except warn me if someone tried to use magic on me or approached, but even that small bit of supernatural protection made me feel very slightly better.

"Tess," I whispered, reaching into my mind for

her memories.

She sat on her rock inside a circle of silver, ephemeral and untouched. Another person who was dead and gone. Only her ghost or whatever it was lived on inside me. Who knows? Maybe I was insane.

Samir was here. My nightmare had come into reality. I needed to think shit though, and now I had all night to do it. Sleep would have to wait.

"Time to play fact. What do we know or think we know?" Somehow talking to a ghost in my head made things clearer.

"Samir is still toying with you," Tess said. "He could have killed you."

"You could sound a little less pissy about that," I muttered.

"I died so you could have more strength to defeat him."

"Point taken. Tell me about time travel. How did I do that? You told me it wasn't possible." Thinking about what I'd done pulled up memories of Steve's double death, but I focused on Tess, on her heart-shaped face and sad eyes. Grief had to wait.

"It is possible. With enough power, though until you did that, I didn't think anyone had enough power except perhaps Samir. But it should never be done. It could damage you forever, and it changes the world. You are now living in a different future."

"I don't feel different," I said. I took a deep breath and rubbed my fingers over my talisman. "But what? Thirty seconds of time travel backward made me feel like I'd been trampled by a Tarrasque. Not looking to repeat that." *Repeat that, get it? Har har.*

Tess wasn't amused. She paced inside my head.

"I brought him here," I said, thinking over everything Samir had said to me. "He knew where I was. I was right about my magic drawing him to me, just wrong about the details. I've been wrong about a lot." It was like Three Feathers all over again. Had I learned nothing?

And now he was here. He didn't want Clyde's heart. Okay, he probably wanted it, but it was, as Tess had said before, a diversion. Something to taunt me about and give me hope that this all could end in anything other than my death and the death of everyone I cared about.

Max and Alek were both away. Vivian, the local vet and another of my friends was away as well, seeing her mother in Florida. Brie and Ciaran were in Ireland. So all of them were out of Samir's immediate reach. I hoped.

If Harper had gotten my message, she, the twins, Junebug, and Rose, would be gathered at the Hen House, behind my wards. Which might not help them much, but they were all shifters. Not easy to kill. I wanted to send them away, too. Tell everyone to scatter and leave myself as the last target standing, but I knew they wouldn't go.

"You might need them," Tess said, her voice gentle but her memories carrying a hard edge that stung my mind.

I pushed away those thoughts. I wasn't going to use them if I didn't have to. There had to be a way to lure Samir out. This was Wylde. In winter. The town was small, everybody knew everybody. There weren't a lot of places to hide. I supposed he could have just waltzed in and killed some poor family, taking their house. Damnit. More grim thoughts. Fear and doubt swirled around like a maelstrom and my headache increased. I needed to sleep. I would need strength tomorrow, whatever came.

I turned and put my back to the wall. Wolf materialized and lay next to the mattress, resting her head up on the thin pillow. I combed my fingers through her silky fur and closed my eyes, praying no dreams would come.

The dreams that came for me were more like memories. And in my memories, nightmares walked and pain ruled.

In my memory-slash-nightmare, I stand again in the library in the house on the lake that Samir and I have shared for the last year of my life.

He's gone on a trip, the first time he's left me alone. I'm giddy with the trust but I can't help snooping around. It isn't like Bluebeard, the library isn't off-limits, but he's said there are texts and things I'm not ready for, magic that could be dangerous to learn until I'm strong enough.

Wind blows in over Lake Michigan, bringing the promise of winter ice. The house is warm but I shiver anyway. It feels odd to be alone. Isolated out here. The houses nearest ours are empty for the winter, and the phone only works when it wants to. I grow bored of watching The Princess Bride *for the twentieth time.*

I'm going to wear out the VHS if I'm not careful.

So library it is. I love the feel of the room, like knowledge is oozing from every polished mahogany shelf. Heavy brass lamps with Tiffany glass line the walls and there are overstuffed leather chairs facing a marble fireplace. And books. Some in cases to protect them, so old that the pages aren't paper but vellum. I can almost smell the ink.

There's one line of shelves that draw me, on the wall farthest from the door. The spines of the books are plain leather, no titles or embossment. Some are stacked in a temperature-controlled case, but there is a row, at least twenty books, that are newer and just resting on the shelf. Journals. I've seen Samir writing sometimes at night when he thinks I'm asleep. It's cute how he nibbles on the tip of his pen, sending covert glances my way with half-slit golden eyes. He keeps a diary. I am glad, it makes him less enigmatic, makes him seem more human. More normal.

Curiosity killed the cat, *I think, but remember that satisfaction brought it back, and reach for one. I almost expect them to be warded, but there's nothing. A thrill goes through me. I know I shouldn't look. I'd be pissed if he read mine. I mean, if I kept one, which I don't.*

Sheepish, I glance around. Still alone. No lightning bolt from the sky has come down on me. This diary looks older and I crack it open. The date reads nineteen-twenty-seven.

The language is a mix of Latin, Coptic, and Avestan. I'm impressed he knows them. Without my weird talent for languages, there is no way I could read this. I doubt anyone could other than Samir. I wonder exactly how old he is. He told me he was born before Jesus once, but he said it in a joking way, and I'd brushed it off. Suddenly I'm not so sure.

Curiosity and fascination overrule propriety. I ache to know him better, to learn the things he hints at but won't say. I'll beg forgiveness later, if I even tell him. I go over to the chairs and curl up, deciding if I'm in for a penny, I might as well shove all in.

Six hours and ten journals later, I flee the house in the dark, my heart in my throat and horror filling my soul.

Because I know one thing, a pattern I read over and over and cannot ignore.

Samir is a monster. Samir is going to kill me, eat my heart, and take my power.

The dreams shift. Me running. Getting afraid. Calling him. Demanding an explanation. Unable to tell him how I knew, but hearing the smooth lie in his voice as he tried to soothe me.

I ran home. Home to Ji-hoon, Sophie, Todd, and Kayla. I doomed them.

Fire. The building is burning. Odd black crystals are strewn across the floor of the old school. I run down the same hallways I always run down in this nightmare. I've dreamed it before. A part of me will always be trapped on this night, trying to reach my family before Samir kills them.

The stones have magic. I can hear them. They can hear me. There is some kind of device. I hear them talking. They think it will go off when I open the door, taking us all down. Ji-hoon thinks he can reach the door, get it open before I get there. Set off the bomb. I'm screaming at them to wait even as I hear them taking a vote.

"Live, Jess," Sophie screams. "Run and live."

"We love you," Ji-hoon says in Korean.

The world explodes. Ash and tears are all that is left

me as the dream fades and I'm still screaming, screaming that I can save them, screaming until all that is left are words and ghosts.

Sheriff Lee's voice pulled me from my nightmares and her hand gripping my shoulder yanked me out of the smoke and debris in my head.

My throat felt raw and my eyes and cheeks were wet. I'd been crying in my sleep. Maybe screaming, too.

"You were calling out in Korean," Lee said, staring at me with curious eyes. "Bad dream?"

The vestiges of the dream still clung to me. Ji-hoon's voice. Sophie seconding his decision. The bomb going off and the whole world collapsing around me.

"Something like that," I said, sitting up. "Is that

coffee? What time is it?"

"Just past eight," she said, handing me the mug. "I hope you don't mind, but I went by your place and got you some clothes. I've got your phone and wallet also—I figured you might want them once Perkins springs you. They are still plowing out the main road, but court should open at noon."

Four more hours.

"Are the phones working yet?" I asked after taking a sip of the coffee and frying the taste buds off my tongue.

"Land line is still irregular, but they have the cell tower working." She set a duffel bag I recognized as mine next to the bed.

"Can I make a call?" I set down my mug on the floor and then opened the bag. She'd brought me a full change of clothes, right down to underwear. I felt a bit weird about that, since I didn't know Lee all that well. Hell, I wasn't even sure what her first name was.

"Not supposed to, but nobody has to know," Lee said with a smile. "Want a donut, too? You can change back here; the camera is only on the hallway."

"What is your first name?" I asked her. "Or

should I just keep calling you sheriff?"

"Rachel," she said.

"Are you in trouble because of me?" I thought back to things that Dick and Balls had said the night before.

"No, not you. Stupid paper-pushing bullshit. This county has always run a little differently, on account of the special nature of many of our citizens. Some people who shouldn't have are starting to take notice. It'll blow over. Always does."

"I'm sorry," I said. "I know this situation isn't helping."

"You didn't kill Steve, did you?" She stared at me evenly, her face unreadable.

"What? No."

"Then this is also not your fault. We'll find the man who did. You focus on staying safe, all right?"

She left then, hopefully to go get me a donut and my phone. I gulped down more coffee and did the world's fastest clothing change. It felt good to be pulling on my own socks, to have a body clean of blood and clothes that smelled only of Tide detergent.

I was going to focus on staying safe. Sort of.

Mostly I wanted the hell out of here so I could track down Samir and do terrible things to him. Starting and ending with ripping out his fucking heart. I didn't say any of that to Rachel as she returned with an Old Fashioned and my cell.

Hoping that Harper and the crew were at the Henhouse plotting Samir's doom with brilliant ideas, safe in front of a nice fire, I punched in a number and held my breath. My phone had two tiny bars of reception but Harper picked up on the second ring.

"Jade? Are you out of jail?" Harper's voice was the best salve to my ruined nerves.

"No, not yet. Perky is coming later to get me. I should be out by one or so. Where are you guys? Is everyone okay?"

"I'm at the college with Ezee and Levi. We got snowed in, but I warned Mom and Junebug. Talked to them about half an hour ago. They are at the Henhouse, but in the spare room in the barn, just in case."

So much for my hopeful vision of all my friends together around a roaring fire plotting revenge.

"Is it true," Harper said then, her voice getting quieter. "Steve?"

"Yeah," I said just as softly, my throat closing up again. "Samir killed him. I tried to stop it, Harper. I did."

"I know you did," she said. "Lee said you were half dead when they brought you in. She was real worried but I figured if you weren't dead, you weren't dying, so I called Perky."

"That's because you are the best," I said. "You should have seen the two jerks I got stuck with. It was like a bad ripoff of *The Closer*. Perky shut them down hard."

We were both silent for a moment, me thinking about Steve and what I would do next, Harper thinking about who knew what.

Harper broke the silence first. "Alek is on his way back. He was trying to get a seat on stand-by when I called him last night."

I felt a twinge of guilt. Maybe I should have tried to call Alek first, but he was supposed to be across the country and safe. Damnit.

"I haven't called him yet. I will." Rachel was giving me the eye from the hallway where she stood pretending not to overhear us. "Look, I am not supposed to have a phone and I don't want to get the sheriff in trouble. I'll call you again as soon as I'm out. Get everyone together and stay safe. I don't know what Samir will do next, but he'll come after us again. This is going to get worse."

"Of course it is," Harper said. "It's the boss fight."

I could almost hear her attempt at a smile. "We'll get him," I said with more conviction than I felt. "For Steve."

"For Steve," Harper said, her voice grim.

After that, there was nothing more to say.

Alek's phone went straight to voice mail. I tried not to let it worry me. If he was on a plane, it would be off, right? Nope, not worried at all. I wanted him away from danger, but I also knew he was a badass who could handle himself. If yesterday had taught me anything, it was that going up against Samir wasn't going to be as simple as "throw a lot of magic at him and win." He wasn't playing fairly.

He'd isolated me. I was sure he'd waited until I was alone in my shop. I had a suspicion he was behind the trouble with the building and Brie's shop. I doubted he had anything to do with Fey business, but the timing was suspicious as well. Maybe he was behind Alek going to New Orleans. It was hard to quell my paranoid thoughts as I sat alone in the jail cell and waited for Kate Perkins to come bail me out.

When she showed up, she wasn't alone, and I knew from the look on her face that something had happened.

Rachel unlocked my cell and motioned for me to come out. Out in the bull pen, Kate Perkins stood talking to two new detectives. I assumed they were detectives, anyway, from how they stood and the clothing they were wearing.

One was a Hispanic male, somewhere in his thirties, with short brown hair and watchful, heavy-lidded brown eyes. He wore a navy-blue suit without a tie, the cut and material of which was understated but had clearly been tailored for him. He kept in shape from the way he filled it out. I saw no badge, but he was carrying a gun in a shoulder holster under the suit jacket. I'd lived with Alek enough to recognize the shape.

His partner was a stout white woman in her fifties, crow's-feet and worry lines clashing with the laugh lines in her sharp face. Her hair was also cut short and iron grey. She had on a thick sweater and dark jeans, with her badge and gun clipped to her belt. She looked me over with a cool, assessing gaze, and I couldn't tell if she liked what she saw.

I followed Rachel over to them. We were the only ones in the building and it felt strangely subdued. A shiver of foreboding crawled up my spine but I shoved it away. I wasn't handcuffed, and at least Dick and Balls weren't here with their accusing, closed-minded looks. Things could've been worse.

"What happened?" I asked as I stopped next to Kate.

"They are dropping the charges." She had her hip up on one of the cluttered desks and a grim look on her face.

"They?" I said, jerking a thumb at the two new people. The scent of mint tickled my nose in a way that wasn't natural. Magic was present. I focused on the woman, but didn't probe at her with my own magic. She had some kind of ward on, centered on a simple silver cross around her neck. Things were getting interesting again quickly.

"I am Senior Detective Hattie Wise," the woman

said. "Everyone just calls me Hattie." She nodded to the man and added, "And this is Special Agent Salazar."

"Special agent? You FBI or something?" I looked the man over again.

"Something like that," he said with a bland smile.

"So where are Dick and Balls?" I asked.

"Jade," Kate admonished with a discreet cough, hiding a grin behind her hand.

"Dick and…" Hattie threw back her head and laughed from her belly. "Oh, I'm going to remember that one."

"Hattie is their supervisor with the Staties," Kate said.

"My sympathies," I said.

"We're sorry about the mistake," Hattie said, sobering quickly. "You *are* free to go, but we were hoping you would come with us instead."

"There's been another murder, just like your friend's," Salazar added.

Time stopped as my stomach turned into a twisting rope and the room started to spin.

"Who?" I'd just talked to Harper an hour ago. She had said everyone was safe. Alek? *No no no, not him.*

Not any of them. Please merciful Universe please.

"Jade. Breathe, Jade," Kate was saying over and over as she gripped my arm. "It was the librarian, Peggy Olsen."

"Peggy? But I hate her," I blurted. At the look on Salazar's and Hattie's faces, I probably should have kept that tidbit to myself. "I mean, she's not someone Samir should go after. He wants to hurt me. Killing people I don't like makes no sense." I couldn't make it line up. Peggy seemed like such a random choice, unless he was just killing everyone I'd come in contact with. I really hated that thought and shoved it away into the throw-up-over-later file.

"You witnessed the first murder. We'd like you to come see the second scene. Maybe you can help us figure out why this man is doing this? Kate said you know him," Hattie said.

"I did. A long time ago. He's stalked me for years. I thought he was here to kill people I care about before coming for me, but... Peggy? Makes no sense." I shook my head. More death. I hadn't liked her, but she didn't deserve this. "Are you sure it was him?"

Murders didn't happen here that often, though

we'd had our share this last year, some perpetrated by yours truly, but there was a chance that Peggy had hexed the wrong person or something and this was unrelated.

"The coroner is waiting with the body. She was killed early this morning or late last night. He says it was the same kind of wire used yesterday on your friend. I think it would be too big a coincidence, no?" Salazar said.

I took a deep breath and nodded. It was clear that I was now free to go because this murder had been committed while I was locked up in here. I was now doubly glad I hadn't blasted my way out last night, though the illogical part of me wished I could have stopped Samir from hurting another person. He'd gone after Peggy for some reason, and as much as I loathed the idea of seeing another crime scene, of seeing anything that would remind me of Steve's horrific death, I needed information. Samir was still way out ahead of me, and if I was going to pwn this boss fight, as Harper would put it, I needed all the tiny advantages I could muster.

"All right," I said. "Let me grab my stuff and I'll go with you. I want to help if I can."

Rachel brought me my coat, wallet, and shoes as I gathered up the duffel bag and said goodbye to the holding cell for what I prayed was forever. I thanked her again and then whispered, "You might want to get your family out of town for a few days, and warn the pack to stay away."

She leaned in and searched my face with troubled eyes. "How bad is this?"

"Bad," I said. "Samir is a sorcerer."

"Fuck," she said. She took a deep breath and tucked her chin down. "Take care of yourself, Jade Crow. Us wolves haven't forgotten what you did for us. Wylde's pack is here if you need us."

I nodded and blinked back a tear. I needed all the help I could get, but I wasn't going to use the shifters as cannon fodder. I'd figure a way out of this, find a way to face Samir again one on one and beat him.

I didn't have any other fucking choice.

Hattie and Salazar were already outside, sitting in a huge black SUV. The day was overcast but the snow had stopped. Someone had shoveled the stairs and snow piled in dirty drifts up to my waist. I climbed into the back seat and buckled my seatbelt. The SUV looked like it could handle the roads, at least.

"So," I said as we pulled out of the parking lot and onto the main road, "which one of you is Mulder?"

Peggy the librarian lived on the south side of town in a housing suburb called Dogwood Park. The park in question was a single block wide and two blocks long, with a playground now buried under a couple feet of fresh snow. The play structure stuck up from the snow like a lurking beast, red-painted metal glinting like spilled blood where the snow hadn't covered it. Peggy's two-story bungalow backed up to the park. It was easy to spot, because there were two police cars, about twenty neighbors in bathrobes and parkas, and a shitload of yellow crime scene tape.

I was surprised our local news station wasn't on it, but things around Wylde had a habit of not getting reported in a timely manner. People here liked their peace and quiet, for very good reason. This was supposed to be a sanctuary for the supernatural, a place they had existed more or less peacefully for over a century.

Until I showed up. I mentally stuck another black X in the "I suck" column, then tried to shrug it off.

"You coming?" Salazar asked me.

I took another deep breath of cold air and nodded. I didn't want to walk into that house. No more crime scenes. No more death. There was too much of it in my life.

But I had to know why Peggy had been targeted. There were pieces in play I didn't see yet, that much was obvious. Samir wanted to fuck with me, to fuck up my life, kill my friends, and just win the award for ultimate evil ex-boyfriend. I wanted to kill him, because that was the only way any of this would end. To do that, I had to get the bastard to stand still and fight me.

And to do that, I had to find him. Had to figure out what he was doing, and why.

Peggy's house smelled like mint, rosemary, and death. I stretched out my magical senses and saw where her wards had been smashed apart. There were broken lines of fine dust, powdered herbs, perhaps, along the windowsills. Motes of it still swirled. She'd tried to protect herself, but I couldn't tell if they were normal everyday wards or if she'd been afraid of something. Someone.

The front entry divided into three rooms with a narrow staircase leading up. The room at the back looked like a small bathroom. To the right was the kitchen. To the left, the living room.

That was where Peggy had died. A deputy gave us little booties for our feet after we stamped the snow off, and I pulled a pair of latex gloves from the offered carton. I didn't want to touch anything, but this was a crime scene, so it was better to be careful. A tall, gaunt white man stood wearing scrubs, waiting by the body. I assumed he must be the coroner.

Blood misted a nice set of blue and white porcelain vases. The carpet was a soft earth tone with a very subtle maple leaf pattern in it. One of the pictures, an oil painting of a black cat and a vase of wild irises, was crooked on the far wall. There was no television, just a coffee table, two linen-colored

ANNIE BELLET

stuffed chairs, and a Victorian-style brown couch.

My eyes took in these details in stutter step, skipping around the room, looking at everything but the body sprawled on the other side of the coffee table. I forced myself to look, trying to see Peggy and not relive Steve's murder.

She lay on her back, arms wide, legs together and bent to the side slightly tucked beneath her, as though she'd been kneeling and fallen backward. Her throat was open, the wire still embedded in the wound. Her hair was loose around her head, partially matted with blood. I hadn't realized how long it was, since she had always had it tucked into a tidy bun every time I'd seen her. There was something nobody had mentioned yet, however. I moved closer to the body, trying not to step in blood.

"She's dressed," Hattie commented.

"And her chest has been blown open, maybe by a gun?" Salazar added. He glanced behind him at the coroner. "Nobody mentioned that."

"Didn't want to touch anything till you got here," the coroner said. "And we didn't find a gun."

I felt like I was caught in a cop movie again listening to the two of them. I turned a manic giggle

86

into a cough.

"You gonna vomit, don't do it on my crime scene," Hattie said, glaring at me. I think she knew I wasn't about to vomit.

I forced away the crazy thoughts, the unreality of the last twenty-four hours, and made myself look at Peggy. Grey edges of rib bone were visible through her mangled blue sweater. Unidentifiable lumps of lung and whatever else we carry around in our chest cavities gleamed wetly in the morning light spilling through the sheer curtains. I didn't need to touch her to know what had happened.

"Her chest wasn't blown open. There was no gun. I think you'll find someone removed her heart." It almost physically hurt to say the words aloud, but life was going from worse to worser and down the hand-basket express to worstest.

"Fuck," Hattie said very softly as she reached up and rubbed her own chest in an almost unconscious gesture. Her expression told me she knew exactly what a missing heart meant.

The coroner took the four steps to get to me and bent over the body. He probed the open chest wound and I turned my head. I didn't need to watch that. It was like someone mixing gravel and Jell-O.

"She's right, heart is missing. I'll be damned."

You and me both, dude, I thought, but kept it to myself. I looked at Hattie and flicked my eyes to the others in what I hoped was an obvious way. I couldn't tell her much with everyone standing around. I didn't know who was a normal or not. I had a sneaking suspicion that Salazar wasn't, but he'd done nothing overtly that said Supernatural-R-Us.

"Dan, why don't you go get some fresh air. Take the deputy with you. Too many bodies in here. I'll call you back in when we're ready for the processing, all right?" Hattie said.

Dan, the coroner, raised a salt-and-pepper eyebrow but shrugged and left. We waited until the front door had closed behind them before Hattie nodded to me.

"Start talking," she said.

"What about?" I asked, jerking my head at Salazar. I moved away from Peggy's body as I did, putting my back to the wall with the least amount of blood on it and facing so that I wouldn't have to see her lying there if I was careful about it.

"I'm an eagle," he said, obviously expecting that

to make sense to me.

Which, sad to say, it totally did. Shifter it was. Right.

"You?" I asked Hattie. "Witch?"

She snorted. "That's me, though my fellow officers like to use a B instead of the W most of the time. And you?"

I was surprised no one had told her. It was pretty much an open secret what I was these days, ever since I went toe to toe with a corrupt shifter Justice a couple months back.

"So you don't talk to the Wylde coven much?" I asked, dodging the question for just a moment longer. I didn't know how they were going to react to what I had to tell them. I wasn't sure how much I even should. I needed more information before I spilled my guts.

I really had to stop thinking about spilling guts. Stat. I swallowed bile and focused on my gloved hands for a moment.

"No," Hattie said after exchanging a glance with Salazar. "I'm a solo practitioner. Never much cared for politics. I have to play them enough in my job as it is."

I took another deep breath and regretted it as mint and blood and urine soaked my senses. Samir had killed Peggy for a reason, all right. He was harvesting hearts. He would have taken her power, minimal though it was, and all her knowledge. He'd know everything she knew, have access to all her memories, if my experience with heart-nomming was any guide to go on. I had to talk to her coven, to warn them. I'd only seen them all together once, when I went and laid down the new threefold law about fucking with me and my friends. I'd recognized a few faces then, but names were eluding me. Shit.

"Jade?" Hattie prompted. "What's going on here?"

"And don't feed us a line. This is serious. There's going to be human heat on these killings and we need to stop them before it gets too big to manage." Salazar moved a couple of steps toward me, his eyes intent on my face.

I made myself look back at Peggy. Samir had done this. He would keep doing this, or maybe worse. I had to stop him, and I clearly wasn't going to be able to do it alone. Keeping the truth from Hattie and Salazar would just get them hurt if they went after

Samir without knowing. I could almost hear Alek's voice in my head telling me that the truth was a good thing, and suddenly I missed him like hell. He'd know what to do; he'd have stood here with me, solid and warm and smart.

And he'd have told me to trust, to take the leap and give these people whatever information I had. To save lives if I could.

I pushed back my longing for Alek, and nodded slowly. "Let me explain," I said with a slight smile. "No, there is too much. Let me sum up."

Not *Princess Bride* fans, these two, because neither gave any sign they recognized the line. So much for trying to smooth things. I sighed.

"Samir, the man who did this? He's a sorcerer. And so am I."

We moved to the kitchen and sat on Peggy's chairs. There was a cold cup of tea with the bag still in it on the kitchen table. I tried not to think about her last moments and instead let the words spill out of me as I gave Hattie and Salazar a rough sketch of what I thought was going on and who the players were.

My story summed up was pretty thin and sad, even to my own ears. There was so much I had to leave out, partially because a lot of it would implicate me in a metric butt-load of crimes, and partially because that stuff might be a distraction. The important thing was that they understood how dangerous Samir was, and that he wasn't going to stop.

"Summers!" I said, breaking off what I had been saying about Samir in mid-sentence as I remembered the name of one of the women in Peggy's coven. "Joyce Summers. She runs a no-kill shelter, Pet Haven. I saw her at the coven meeting. She'll know who the rest are. Do you have Peggy's phone? They'll all be in there, I bet."

"One moment," Hattie said. Both she and Salazar were sitting on the edge of their chairs, not writing anything down, just staring at me with grim faces. "The heart-eating thing, it's real? It really works that way?"

"Yes," I said. "All the horror stories you might have heard about sorcerers? They are probably all about Samir. If he's decided to gain power and knowledge by eating the witches, he's going to keep going until we're down thirteen women." I didn't know why he was doing it. They hadn't been that powerful, but maybe it was more than what their magic could add. Memories and experiences, I knew firsthand, were powerful things in their own right.

"How many hearts have you eaten?" Salazar asked, his tone deceptively light compared to the intense look in his eyes. His gaze was very eagle-like, now that I thought about it, and I felt like a mouse under it.

I was no mouse. "How long have you been beating your wife?" I shot back, folding my arms over my chest.

One corner of his mouth lifted and he inclined his head. "Fair enough," he said in a way that told me this wasn't a conversation either of us wanted to have. "It was a poorly phrased question."

"Look," I said, relenting a little. "Hypothetically and off record and all that, if I did kill anyone ever in my life? It would only be because they were trying to kill me first." Which was mostly true. Ignoring the times it hadn't been true. But partial truth was still like being honest, right? Baby steps.

"I have to call my boss," Salazar said. "If it is as you say, this is going to get much worse."

He rose and walked up the stairs, leaving Hattie and I sitting, staring at each other.

"I never thought your kind were quite real. Even living in Wylde all my life. I guess this place attracts all things eventually." She shook her head.

"Thank you for not freaking out and hating me

just for being what I am," I said. Which wasn't exactly what I meant, but she seemed to understand.

"You haven't given me cause. I've been on this job too long to judge things by their reputation anymore. And the worst I've seen? It was done by humans to humans. The normals do more damage to themselves than the supernatural ever could."

Supernaturals could be pretty damn bad, but I didn't say that aloud. I thought about Bernard Barnes and the rotting wolves he'd been magically freezing and using as batteries, and shivered, rubbing my hands along my arms. The latex gloves snagged on my sleeves weirdly and reminded me I was at a crime scene. Sitting in a house with a dead woman who used to hate me.

"So the wire, you said it was magic?" Hattie said after a couple of silent minutes.

"It was when he used it on… my friend." I had trouble getting Steve's name out. It felt too real to say it aloud, like invoking his death. "I tried to get in the way, and it went right through me. I think it has to be driven by his power, and only works on the target. Made my throat raw as hell, though—I could barely talk for hours."

"Tried to get in the way? So he threw it, not used it like a garrote?"

"Yeah, it just flew through the air." I touched my neck. "Right through me."

"He could have killed you then?" Hattie had her inscrutable cop face back on.

"I think so," I said. I hadn't mentioned Wolf. No point even trying to explain that part. It didn't matter. I'd been so weak, so distraught. I'd almost wanted to die just so it would end. Not a thought I wanted to dwell on in that moment. Or ever.

"He said he wasn't 'bored enough yet,'" I added. I caught her gaze with mine and leaned forward. "He's evil, detective. Pure selfish evil."

Salazar came down the stairs with an annoyed look on his face. He waved off our questioning glances and pressed his lips together. "Let's get the coroner in to handle the scene. Crime scene folk have arrived, too. Is there any magic around we should be aware of?"

I pulled on my magic, letting my senses stretch out. The broken wards were fainter now. I sensed none of Samir's sickly sweet magic.

"I think it's safe," I said.

Hattie let the deputy and coroner back in. She

started questioning the deputy about the scene while Salazar looked around for Peggy's phone. I hung out in the kitchen, feeling useless and tired. I decided to call Harper and went to get my phone from my jacket where it was hung in the hall. I would see if Alek was back yet, and make sure everyone was okay, but as I pulled out my phone, Hattie reappeared with the deputy in tow.

"What was the name of that friend of the victim's?" she asked.

"Joyce Summers, I think, why?" I slid my phone into my jeans pocket. *Please don't say she's dead, please don't say she's dead, please don't say it.*

"Yeah, that's the one," the deputy said, running a hand through thinning his thinning hair.

"She's the next-door neighbor. She's over there right now waiting to give an official statement," Hattie said. "Joyce Summers is the one who found the body."

Joyce Summers wasn't someone I'd said more than four or five words to in all the years I'd been in

Wylde, but I'd known who she was because of my dealings with Vivian Lake, the local vet, and because Harper had a serious soft spot for stray animals. Joyce was in her fifties, with brown hair that was too evenly colored to have gotten that brown by natural means and skin so pale the veins in her cheeks showed through like rivers on a map. Her eyes were puffy as she greeted us with the perfunctory stiffness of someone going into mild shock and showed us where to hang our coats.

From the smell alone, it was easy to tell that Joyce loved and owned a lot of pets, but while it was noticeable, it wasn't that overwhelming. It smelled like a house where animals ruled with decorum, musk and coffee underlying the hint of air freshener and mint. Her house was cluttered with comfortable furniture and cat trees, her carpet littered with cat toys. There were at least four of the critters in view, and I gently stroked a big calico cat who was resting on the back of an overstuffed chair.

Joyce did an almost comical double take as Hattie sent the deputy out and the four of us sat down.

"What is she doing here?" she demanded, rousing from her grief-stricken torpor. She pointed a trembling finger at me.

"Saving your ass, I hope," I said.

"Ladies," Hattie said. "Jade is helping us with the investigation. Can you walk us through what happened? Do you know who killed your friend?"

Joyce dropped her hand into her lap and sniffed hard. She started to speak, but stopped and looked at Salazar, then at Hattie with a question on her face.

"I'm Special Agent Salazar," Salazar said in a patient voice. "I'm an eagle shifter and I know what you are already, so you can speak freely."

"We always check on each other after a storm, because we live alone, you see. My husband and I separated recently. He moved out just last month and I'm not used to being on my own. Peggy and I, well, you know. She is our leader." Joyce stopped and sniffed again. She pulled a wadded-up handkerchief out of a drawer in the sewing table next to her and dabbed at her nose.

"I tried to call, but she didn't pick up. I saw lights on and thought maybe she had her phone off. When she didn't answer the door, I just went in. We don't lock our doors much around here, as the detective can tell you, agent," Joyce said.

"And that's when you found her?" Salazar prompted.

Joyce nodded and tears started to leak from her eyes. She dabbed at those, too.

"She was… I mean. Blood. Everywhere. I… I'm sorry. Do I have to talk about this? What is the point? I know who did it." Her expression hardened and she looked at me.

"Wait a minute," I said, holding up my hands in mock surrender. "Don't you even try to pin this on me. I have an airtight alibi." I refrained from saying I'd been locked up in jail all night. Joyce didn't need to know that part.

"Not you," she said. "Though you're the cause all right. It was that golden-eyed demon, Mr. Cartwright. He did this, sure as the sun rises in the east."

I sat back in the chair, disturbing the cat behind me. She got up and jumped down, giving me a look fit to kill. I rubbed my palms on my thighs.

"You know Samir?" I asked. "Do you know why he did this?"

Joyce pressed her lips together into a thin line. She looked at Hattie, then shifted her gaze to Salazar.

When they both were silent, expectant in their expressions and posture, she looked back at me and nodded. I wanted to yank her out of her chair and drag the answers out of her, but I forced myself to be calm. She'd been through a hell of a shock; I could take a moment to be patient.

"You have to understand. We didn't know what was going on. It was just a way to make a little extra money, which the shelter needed. The library too, and Alice's son needed braces, and… well. Extra money isn't something folks like us can turn down." She clutched at her dirty handkerchief like it was a security blanket.

"Money?" I said. "From Samir? For what?"

"For you," she said softly. "He was paying us to keep an eye on you."

"When? How long?" I spat the questions out, my brain spinning.

"Oh gosh. Three years now, at least." Joyce looked down at her hands.

I closed my eyes and wrapped my willpower around my temper. I took a deep breath and tried to think calm thoughts. So Samir had been telling the truth, it seemed. He had known where I was. What I was doing. I might have noticed one or two people watching me. Even in a small town, seeing someone over and over when you aren't friends would start to stand out. But a whole coven? That was thirteen different women, all probably pillars of the community, thirteen spies to rotate around. I thought of how many had kids or relatives they bought games for. How many times I'd run into people at the grocery store or Brie's or one of the pubs.

"You didn't think that was odd?" Hattie asked. "A man paying you to spy on a woman?"

"Oh, we did, a bit. He said he was her father, and up until last year none of us had ever met him. But we all thought Jade was a witch, a solo practitioner like yourself, Hattie. He was just asking for updates on what she did, who she talked to. We figured we were going to keep tabs on her anyway, why not take the money? Peggy promised we would warn Jade if anything happened. Until, well, until we realized what you were."

"Then Peggy tried to run me out of town," I said. "They know, I gave them the basic details."

"She knew you'd bring trouble down on us. We

can't be involved with sorcerers. Nothing good ever comes of that. And now she's dead. He killed her, didn't he? Took her heart. Oh my poor Peggy." Joyce started crying again, sniffling and snorting into her kerchief. A tuxedo cat unwound itself from its perch in a cat tree by the front window and went over to her, pressing himself against her legs.

"We stopped reporting to him," she said after choking back a few more sobs. She scritched the cat's ears. "Is that why he did this? I told her it was a bad idea. I told her."

"You have to get the coven out of town," I said to Joyce, glancing at Hattie and Salazar. The agent and the detective were being very quiet for people interviewing a witness. "He's not going to stop. Samir wants your powers, but I think he really wants your memories, your knowledge."

"Stop saying his name," she whispered, looking around as though he might pop out of the shadows.

"He's not Voldemort," I said more sharply than I meant. "He's a man, an evil, awful person, but still just a man. His name isn't going to summon him. Hell, who fucking knows if it is even his real name?"

"You should never have come here," Joyce said.

"It's about five years too late for that, lady. Have you contacted the rest of the coven? I'm serious. Wylde isn't going to be a safe place for witches for a while." I glanced at Hattie again as I said it. Peggy had known about her; that much was obvious, since Joyce knew who she was. And what Peggy had known, Samir now knew. My brain balked at the possibilities.

"I already activated the phone tree, right after I called nine-one-one and asked for Hattie here." Joyce pulled the cat into her lap.

"How much does Samir know?" I asked her. "What did you tell him about me and my friends?"

"Everything," she said in a whisper, not meeting my gaze. "He knows about the Macnulty girl, her family. Those handsome twins. Your store. We told him whatever details he asked. It was all very mundane, harmless knowledge, really."

I stood up and yanked my phone out of my pocket. This was worse than I'd thought. He had Peggy's memories, but he also had years of reports on me and my new life. Years to get to know where I went, what I did, whom I saw.

Where I went.

Harper. The Henhouse. *Shit.*

As if by fucking magic, my phone rang, playing Harper's song.

I flicked it to answer and put it to my ear as dread turned my stomach into self-animating ropes.

"Jade? They're being attacked. Mom said there were men. At the house. Levi's driving us there. Please, Jade. Come." Harper's voice cracked into a shriek.

"On my way," I said. I jammed my phone into my pocket and crossed the living room. "I need a ride," I said to Salazar and Hattie as they followed me.

"What is it?" Salazar asked as I threw open the front door.

"Samir is attacking my friends. I have to get to the Henhouse B&B, do you know it?" I directed the last part at Hattie as I strode toward the SUV parked outside the crime scene next door.

"I do," she said, huffing as she tromped over the un-shoveled snow, her shorter legs sinking her deeper. "But the roads aren't good, and besides, I can't just leave the crime scene."

I stopped, shivering in the cold air. My coat was

still hanging inside Joyce's house.

"You saying you won't get me there? You won't help me? Don't you want to catch the killer?"

"Jade," Salazar said in a hushed voice, glancing around. No one was still lingering in the cold now that the body had been removed. We stood alone in a tomb-quiet sea of white. "We can't. We're no match for a sorcerer. I've been ordered to spin the story for the humans, and then back down."

So. He was saying it wasn't their fight.

Well, fuck them. They were right. It wasn't their fight.

It was mine.

And I didn't need a damn car. I gathered my magic, power filling my blood, racing along with all the strength of my fear and anger.

I was a motherfucking sorceress and I was going to fly.

I'd never managed to fly before. I could leap and glide, sort of an extended long-jump where I just refused to touch the ground for as long as I could suspend my disbelief and trust my magic to hold me aloft. But flying had been out of my grasp.

No more. I shot into the air a good fifty or sixty feet, Superman-style, one fist thrust ridiculously in front of me, the other clinging with total terror to my D20 talisman. Tears streamed from my eyes and froze to my cheeks until I shoved magic out in front of me, pushing a shield out to block the worst of the wind and the cold.

The landscape was black and white from up here,

houses zipping away beneath me as I hurtled through the air in the general direction of the Henhouse B&B. With the snow covering roads and landmarks, I could only go by the sun and my own sense of direction. The Henhouse had a bright red roof on it, with enough of a slope that I figured some red would show through even with the heavy snowfall.

Horror pictures flickered through my brain. Rose and Junebug strapped to a giant bomb. Samir torturing them. My friends arriving before I did and being cut down by screaming men with giant machine guns. Images of me arriving and finding only silence and everyone dead, bodies laid out, throats open, eyes staring blank and cold at the sun.

I shoved those thoughts away, shoved them into my power, gathered my anger and my fear, and fed it all into the magic. No one was going to die. Only Samir.

A giant plume of black smoke drew my gaze as I soared over the trees. I corrected my course, heart in my throat. The Henhouse was on fire.

I tried to drop down near the clearing where the buildings were burning, but landing proved harder than it looks in the movies. I didn't so much glide down out of the sky as plummet like meteor into the snow.

Fresh powder snow? Not as soft as it looks. Shivering, the wind half knocked out of me, I climbed to my feet and ran toward the burning house. The roof had caved in and taken most of the second floor with it. Acrid smoke, tasting of ash and the sickly sweetness of Samir's magic, filled my nose and mouth. I plunged through the door, yelling for Rose. Paper curled with heat and caught on the walls, the curtains burned, and a huge burning beam dropped as I charged into the entry, cutting off the stairs and living room. I sent my magic out like a wave, trying to feel for life, for anything. Only fire.

"Jade!" Harper's voice reached me through the roar of the blaze and I stumbled free of the house as something else crashed behind me. More beams. The whole place was burning to the ground with a vengeance.

Harper, Ezee, and Levi had just arrived, Levi's four-wheel-drive still steaming in the parking area, his tire chains packed with snow. I stumbled toward them, going for Harper as she tried to rush past me.

"They weren't in the house," I said, remembering.

"No one is there."

I hoped I wasn't lying. The house had felt like no one was alive—no one, not even a shifter, could live through that kind of blaze. If Rose or Junebug were in there, they'd have escaped or already be dead.

"The barn," Harper said. Her expression went from relief back to panic and she turned and bolted for the barn.

The barn wasn't on fire, but it had taken a lot of bullets. The wood was chewed up with hundreds of holes, chunks and splinters sticking out from the doors like spines.

The horses were dead. Something had ripped apart one of them; the other two had died from gunfire. Though my ears rang after the mad flight and the roar of the house fire, the barn felt eerily silent and still.

"Oh God," Harper whispered, looking into each stall, her movements growing more panicked as she went. "Oh God." She slammed shut a stall door and kicked over a bucket, a litany of curses pouring from her mouth as she searched.

My legs felt like lead but I climbed up the ladder into the loft. Sleeping bags were still laying on mounded up hay. A turned over milk crate had a thermos and a stack of playing cards on it. A broken mug lay on the floor nearby. No sign of Harper's mom or Levi's wife. The upper door was open, a rifle on the floor by it. Hay was everywhere.

Something glinted in the hay by the door, too big to be spent casings and too small to be a gun or knife. A cell phone.

"Is that Mom's?" Harper said. Her voice was soft, flat, as though she'd shouted herself out.

I held up the phone. "Yeah," I said. "They aren't here. There aren't any bodies. No blood. Maybe they escaped?"

"In this snow? Junebug could fly off, but Mom couldn't get away without leaving a trail. Come on." She didn't wait for me as she turned and climbed down the ladder.

"Blood," Levi said as we met up with the twins on the side of the barn. "Junebug's."

"How can you tell?" I asked.

"I know my wife," he said grimly.

"No fox tracks?" Harper said, looking around.

The ground here was a mess from boots tramping it down. I was no tracker, but I could recognize boot tread and that many feet had been here. Samir had brought in help. It figured. He'd used people to abduct my family, too. The bastard seemed to hate getting his hands dirty unless he had to.

More information about him, but useless unless I could find a way to turn it to my advantage. I sighed and followed Ezee and Levi through the snow. My skin was turning from brown to blue in the cold and I pumped more magic through myself to keep from shivering.

"Where is your coat?" Ezee asked.

"I left it in town."

The blood droplets ended in the trees, as did the boot tracks. Someone, or maybe two someones had come in here and tried to follow Junebug, but given up quickly.

"Just drops," Ezee said to Levi, rubbing his twin's shoulder reassuringly. "Takes more than a flesh wound to hurt your girl. She's okay."

"Unless they got her," Levi muttered, shaking Ezee's hand off.

"We need to go back, look for where the tracks go."

Something rustled above us and I readied magic,

pooling purple fire in my hand.

Junebug, in owl form, dropped gracefully out of the trees and shifted as she hit the snow, effecting a far better landing than I had. She practically jumped into Levi's arms, tears on her cheeks.

"No point tracking them. They came in snowmobiles," she said, then looked at Harper. "Rosie's gone."

"The house is burning. No one is in the barn," Harper said. "What happened?"

"She made me fly away. I got hit, just a graze," she added quickly as Levi growled. "I didn't want to leave her, but, nobody argues with Rose." Junebug turned imploring eyes on Harper. "She said she'd be right behind. But they had her pinned. I tried to fly back, but two of the men came after me. They took her. There were too many, Harper. I'm sorry."

"No," Harper said, her voice still deadly quiet, as cold as the snow surrounding us. "Not your fault. Was she still alive?"

"Yes," Junebug said. "I heard her swearing at them."

"He'll keep her alive," I said with as much confidence as I could muster. "He'll use her as bait for the rest of us. This is what he did to me before. Taking people I love and hurting them to hurt me."

"So we go get her. And kill him." Harper turned and strode back through the trees.

My cell phone rang. I fumbled it from my jean's pocket. Unknown number. But I knew who it was.

"You fucking bastard," I said as I answered. "Is she alive?"

"Jade, of course she's alive." Samir's slimy, smooth voice was jarring in my ears. I wanted to reach through the phone and rip his heart out from here.

If only I could figure out that spell. Fucker.

"What do you want?" I said, playing the game.

Harper had stopped and turned. Everyone gathered closer, their shifter senses allowing them to hear the phone call just as well as if I'd put him on speaker.

"I want Clyde's heart. It's mine. So nice of you to keep it for me, but I think one life is worth another, no?"

"I give you the heart, you give back Rose? Unharmed?" I ground the words out, looking at Harper.

"Well, she's not entirely unharmed. Put up quite

the fight for an old fox. But she's alive. For now. Bring me the heart, and she can stay that way," Samir said.

I didn't need Alek's power of truth detection to know he was a lying son of a bitch. Harper growled, her lips curling back in a snarl that looked at odds with her human face.

"I don't have the heart," I said. "I don't even know where it is."

"But you know who does," Samir said. It was not a question.

"I do," I said, thinking of Alek. I had no idea where Alek was, however. "It will take some time." I needed to buy us time. Buy Rose time. We had to have a plan, and maybe I could get ahead of Samir, use this to lure him into a trap of my own. Something, anything. I hadn't saved Rose from that evil warlock Barnes just to let her die like this.

"Call this number in two hours. I don't hear from you, it's only her body you'll find." Samir hung up.

I shivered, nearly dropping the phone. Harper wrapped an arm around me and we leaned into each other for a long moment. She was warm and solid and I wanted to hug her forever. To keep her safe, to wipe the anger and sadness from her unhappy face.

"He's not going to release her, is he?" Harper said, pulling away so she could look me in the eye.

I swallowed the giant lump in my throat. "No," I said softly. "He'll find a way to screw up the trade, turn it into a trap."

"It's freezing out here," Ezee said. "The barn still stands. Come on. We can talk and form a plan. We will figure this out."

Glad for someone else taking charge, I followed them back to the barn. Junebug started crying again as she saw the horses. Then she punched a wall so hard the entire barn shuddered and groaned. Levi wrapped an arm around her and spoke in soft tones until she looked like she wasn't about to murder someone, guiding her up the ladder to the loft.

I dragged a sleeping bag around me, glad for the warmth.

"Should we call the fire department? Can they even get out here?" Levi asked.

"No," Harper said. "Let it burn itself out. We can't save the house. The snow will keep it contained."

"At least Max isn't here," I said, trying to find a

silver lining.

"Max," Harper said. She reached into her coat and started to pull out her phone, but stopped. "No. He's safe where he is. If I tell him anything, the idiot might try to come back and help."

"So what do we do now?" Ezee asked.

"Is Steve really dead?" Levi asked at the same time.

"And they thought you did it?" Harper added.

Everyone looked at me. I drew the sleeping bag closer, as though it could shield me from their questioning gazes, from their expectation that somehow I could fix all this.

I had to find a way. This was all my fault.

"Yes," I said. "Samir killed Steve. He also killed Peggy Olsen."

That brought on more questions. I gave them the very rough sketch of what had happened and what I knew.

"Witches were spying on you the whole time and they didn't think that was really fucking creepy?" Harper's voice was almost back to normal, a slow burning anger warming it again.

"Guess not," I muttered. "We have to come up with a new plan, though. Only Alek knows where the heart is. And Samir won't let Rosie go alive anyway. We can't make the trade."

"Yeah, it sounded like Trap Here all over it, just from the tone in his evil fucking voice," Harper said. Relief flooded through me. I had been worried she wouldn't understand why we couldn't just obey the ransom demand.

Alek didn't answer his phone. Straight to voicemail. Ezee started to look worried as I jammed my phone back into my pocket.

"Yosemite isn't around, is he?" I asked him.

Ezee shook his head. "He doesn't exactly carry a phone, but he said he had something to do this week. Related to Brie and Ciaran being out of town, I guess."

"What now?" Levi said. He chewed on his lower lip as he looked over at his twin. "It looks like it is just us."

"Junebug, how many were here? Did you see Samir? He's got dark hair, gold eyes, and is tall, but not as tall as Alek or Yosemite." I turned to Junebug.

"Nobody is as tall as Yosemite," Harper said with a snort. There was color in her cheeks and I hoped that meant she was coming out of shock.

"No," Junebug said. "Nobody like that. There were men, maybe fifteen? Some were shifters. I smelled wolf and bear. The men who came into the woods looking for me were wolves, for sure." She ran a hand through her tangled hair and winced.

Why hadn't Samir even been with them? He'd been confident they could handle the shifters? Had he known that only two were here? It bothered me, but I couldn't work out why it should. He was playing a game, and I didn't have the rulebook. I had two hours to figure out what to do, and time was slipping away as we sat here. Looking around the loft again, my gaze rested on the broken mug. It was earthenware, glazed blue with a green handle.

"Harper," I said as an idea took nebulous shape in my brain. "Did Rose make that mug?"

"What? Oh, yeah, that's one of her oldest ones. Why?" Harper looked at the mug and then back at me.

I left the warmth of the sleeping bag and picked up the biggest intact chunk. Closing my eyes, I focused and pushed my magic into the cup. Harper's mother had thrown the clay, worked it with her hands, given this object form and purpose. Part of her would be infused it in, bonded forever to it through intention and the power of creation. Every cup of coffee she'd drunk from it, every moment it had lived on her shelf and been a part of her day-to-day life would have reinforced the bond.

A bond I could track.

The spell snapped into place and I felt a strong pull to the west. Rose. Alive.

"I can track her," I said. I met four grim faces. "I don't know what we'll find, but she's alive and this mug can take us to her. Maybe we can rescue her."

"You've got my axe," Ezee said.

"And my sword," Levi added.

"That would be a lot more comforting if either of you had weapons, or knew how to use them," I said, my heart lifting at their unquestioning decision that they were in this with me. I didn't want to get them hurt or killed, but I couldn't face down fifteen shifters on my own, rescue the lady, and fight Samir. I needed help. I'd made the decision to stay in Wylde and stop running.

Now it was time to fight.

"We have teeth and claws," Levi said.

"And a rifle," Junebug added. "With the Idaho

State Fair sharpshooting champion to fire it." Her expression was stubborn and stopped any objection Levi might have made. "If I shift, I'll still be injured, so I'm more use in this form. My human isn't bleeding." Her eyes dared Levi to object. He was smarter than that and just nodded and kissed her fiercely on the lips.

"And my magic," I said, feeling the pull of Rose's location. "Once we know where they are keeping Rose, we can form a better plan than 'think positive and get lucky,' all right? So let's drive out of here before someone shows up and tries to arrest me for arson."

With the kind of week I was having, it was totally possible that could happen.

"Think we can win?" Ezee said to me softly as we left the barn and tromped through the dirty, churned-up snow toward Levi's car.

"We're gamers," Harper answered before I could. "We always win."

I prayed to the universe that she was right and clung to the locating spell with every ounce of hope I had left.

The spell led us away from town. Levi found ways to keep us heading more or less straight at it, but we had to drive over roads still clogged with snow, lumbering our way toward an unknown destination.

Nobody talked much. We were alone in our thoughts. I sat up front, focusing on the spell, trying to pinpoint where they might be holding Rose.

"I know where we are going," Ezee said suddenly.

"Old church?" Levi asked.

"I think so. What else is out here? Turn around, go back to Red Rock."

"Old church?" I looked at Levi's profile as he jammed on the brakes and executed a three-point turn in the middle of the road.

"There's an old church, sometimes used as a grange, rented to groups, that kind of thing, just out Red Rock Road. You keep pointing in its direction, more or less. Don't know why I didn't see that."

"Cause I'm prettier and smarter," Ezee said with forced joviality.

"Don't get too close," I said. "They'll probably watch the road."

When we pulled up after following the new road for a mile or so, I couldn't see a church, just a lot of trees lining the roadway. The spell tugged hard, and the road here had been used recently, tire tracks and snow treads were all over it. Levi turned the car around, facing it outward. He looked back at Junebug.

"You are staying here," he said in a tone that brooked no argument. "You keep that rifle ready, because if we come out of there in a hurry, I want you ready to get us out of here."

She made a face but nodded. "I'll set up in the back, and cover your asses," she said.

I shivered in the chill air as we climbed out, the weak winter sun doing nothing to warm up the day.

At least Rachel had brought me my hiking boots and wool socks, so my feet weren't as miserable as the rest of me. Jeans and a long-sleeve shirt with no coat was shitty winter wear.

Pushing aside my discomfort, I let the anticipation of getting to do something, anything, to strike back at Samir warm me.

"Here," Harper said. "Take my coat. It's not great for this, but better than just your shirt." She slipped out of her quilted leather jacket and handed it over.

"But won't you be cold?" I asked, taking it anyway.

"I have fur," she said. "That spell say Mom is in there?"

I refocused on the chunk of mug in my hands. "Yes, definitely close," I said.

Levi, Ezee, and Harper all shifted to their animal forms as we headed into the woods. It was easier going beneath the trees. The thick canopy had stopped a lot of the snow, and as long as I avoided the tree wells, I never sank more than ankle deep. We reached the edge of the trees without hearing or seeing anyone.

The church had probably been built sometime

around the turn of the nineteenth century and not updated much since. It was a squat, grey rectangular building with narrow windows and heavy wooden doors. I saw no movement around the building. Coyote-Ezee, his brown body low to the snowy ground, crept along the edge of the parking lot the rest of us waited hidden in the tree line. No one fired at him. Snowmobiles, four of them, were pulled up under a carport that was definitely a late add-on to the church. Those were the only vehicles, which bothered me. Coyote-Ezee made his way to them, running low and fast over the ground. He crouched for what felt like eternity next to the door, so still I could barely make him out.

Finally, he slipped away from the church, made a quick circuit of the clearing, and came back around to us. We pulled back quietly into the trees and everyone shifted back to human. I let go of the locating spell and tucked the ceramic fragment into Harper's coat.

"Anything?" Levi asked.

"At least three inside, I could hear them talking. I don't think they are expecting anything. There's definitely a bear in there." Ezee took a deep breath and looked at me.

"Have you guys been inside this place?" I asked.

"Yeah." Levi answered. "It's pretty much a big room up top, with a side office space. Then it has a basement, which is where the kitchen is, with a couple bathrooms in back."

"Windows or doors downstairs?" Harper asked.

"Some narrow windows near the ground, but they'll be pretty well snowed under if they aren't boarded up for the winter. There's a storm door in back, leads down to the hall by the bathrooms, if I remember right. No windows in the bathrooms."

I nodded. "Rose isn't going to stay in there easily. I bet they've got her downstairs."

"Makes sense. Locked in a bathroom. That's where I would put someone. Only one door, no windows, mostly underground. She won't be able to get out easily." Harper nodded along with me.

"Is your evil ex-boyfriend here?" Ezee asked.

"I don't know," I said. "This feels weird to me, like we're missing something. Only four snowmobiles? Where are the rest of the people who attacked the Henhouse?"

"It's a trap?" Levi said.

"What time is it?" I asked, even as I pulled out my phone and checked. We had less than an hour until Samir's deadline. "He's had an hour since we talked, bit more, to go elsewhere, or send people to try to find me? I don't know."

"Your spell said Mom is here. I'm going in, trap or not." Harper folded her arms over her sweater, glaring at me.

"We're not warriors," I said. "You are shifters, sure, but we aren't exactly equipped for battle. These guys could be mercenaries or something."

"What did we do when that warlock guy tried to kill Mom and Ezee?"

"Fought him," I said. "Well, I saved your asses, anyway." I tried to grin, but my face didn't want to obey.

"And the undead guy who tried to wipe out your people? What happened to him?"

"He's dead," I said, "But I didn't kill him. I just freed the spirit that did it."

"And when the ninja assassin came to take you out?"

"I killed him," I said, my voice softer now.

"And that corrupt Justice who tried to blow up all

the wolves?" Harper raised her chin and stared me down. "Or those two sorcerers who showed up to take us all out and summon a super-evil Irish badass with slavering hell-beasties?"

"Okay," I said, seeing her point. "You're right. We should be glad that there are fewer people here, I guess, and that they are just shifters, eh? We'll worry about Samir later. Let's go get Rosie."

The plan we worked out, crouched there in the snow, was stupidly simple. I'd walk toward the front doors and do a lot of showy magic, keep myself shielded against bullets, and create a nice distraction. Levi, Ezee, and Harper would go around and break in the storm doors, searching the lower level for Rose first and then coming up the front to meet me or running away out the back if they found her.

I'd destroy the snowmobiles or maybe steal one, and meet them back at the car. Or fly away, which was my super backup plan, now that I knew I could fly. Of course, if I flew, I'd have to land again, and I wasn't in a super hurry to repeat that experience.

Unless Samir was here. I had no idea how I was going to fight him, but at least out here I could unleash some real magic and not have to worry about taking the town out with me. If he was here, well, things were going to get very dangerous. For him.

One problem at a time, I told myself. First, I had to go get the attention of people with guns.

I'd marched up on dudes with guns before, so I had a weird feeling of déjà vu. This time, however, I wasn't going to waltz in under a fake flag of truce. This time, I was going in magic blazing. If I could figure out how.

Pulling my power into a shield was second nature now so I was pretty sure I could stop bullets from making me into a colander. If I'd had time to stop and think about it, I would have been impressed with how much magic I was able to toss around these days. The training was paying off.

Those kinds of thoughts just led to thinking about my failure to save Steve, so I shoved them away as soon as they surfaced and concentrated on my path toward the main door. There was about twenty yards of open ground to cover.

Unless I didn't go through the door. Rule number

one of adventuring? Always look up. The counterpart of that is mistake number one of horror movie survival, which is never looking up.

The roof of the church was sloped, but not super steep. There was a bell tower that was boarded up with a metal spike on it that might have been a weathervane sometime in the previous century. Thick snow coated the roof in drifts, and parts had sloughed off with their own weight, but there was enough in piles that I thought I could effect a landing without breaking my legs.

Time to fly again.

"Okay, when I land on the roof, make a break for the back door," I said to my friends.

"Land on the roof? What?" Harper looked at me like I was crazy.

I probably was. I felt a little crazy. Glad to be out of jail and doing something, anything, to strike back at Samir. To act instead of react.

I grinned at her. "Just watch, grasshopper."

I threw myself into the air before I thought about how stupid my plan was, crashing upward through the trees. Branches slapped my face, evergreen needles catching and tangling in my braid. Snow went right down the back of my jacket, bringing out a yelp of surprise that I quickly swallowed. I hurtled a good hundred feet up and pulled downward with my magic to stop myself. I hung in the air, feeling pretty pleased. Jade Crow: one, gravity: zero.

A coyote, a wolverine, and a fox, all about twice or more the size of the wild version, glided through the forest and got into position below me. From up here, I could see the SUV, though not Junebug.

Shouting rang out from inside and the front door of the church opened. A man in a grey and white camouflage coat emerged, looking toward the trees I'd just sailed out of. He was a shitty adventurer, but a great horror movie victim. He scanned the treeline but missed the floating woman in the sky. If I'd been closer and more sure of the angle, I would have *Magic Missiled* his ass.

He went back inside, and I flew toward the church, angling my descent to hit the biggest lump of snow on the roof. This landing went much better, as I used my magic like a jetpack, pulling myself toward the target spot, then pushing away as I came close so that my descent slowed. Thinking about it like thrusters in a science fiction movie helped a ton.

I'd never been a huge fan of Mandalorians from *Star Wars*, but the jetpack thing was suddenly a whole lot cool-seeming.

If only I'd had badass body armor, too. And a lightsaber.

Instead, I had magic. I hit the roof and let out a whoop as I thumped down. I wrapped my power around me in a shield in case the idiots started shooting through the roof and kept making lots of noise.

Voices and then bodies appeared. Two men charged out, guns in their hands, pointing and yelling at me. They took shots but I glided forward, using my magic to keep me just over the snow and to hold my balance on the ridge of the church. Their shots went wild, one glancing off my shield but the others missing me by what felt like miles.

Then one of the men shifted, turning into the biggest black bear I hoped ever to see. He let out a roar and jumped, flying upward through the air and gaining the lower edge of the roof. It held his weight. Not good. I threw a wave of force at him, slamming the bear off the roof edge, and back to the snow below.

Counterforce is a bitch, apparently. My push knocked me backward, and I lost concentration as I rolled down the other side of the roof. Wrapping magic around me, I rolled through the thick snow and gained my feet as the giant bear rounded the side of the church and flew at me. Snow melted off my face as I rubbed my hands over myself quickly, checking for injury. My jeans and coat were soaked and I knew I'd be a human icicle if I stood still out here like this long enough. No danger of that. I heard more gunfire and braced for impact, but it was muffled. Coming from the other side of the church, or perhaps inside. I hoped it wasn't from inside.

I had big-ass bear trouble to worry about. Harper and the twins would have to handle their own problems.

The bear charged, and I threw lightning from my hands. It fizzled and arced away from the shifter. Damn.

Time for fire. This much cold and wet, and the church being mostly stone, I didn't have to worry about burning down the forest or the building. I threw a fireball right into the bear's face from nearly point-blank range. He roared in pain and rage and sprang aside, plunging his burning body into the snow. Acrid smoke steamed off him as he twisted and came to his feet again, snarling.

Okay. Maybe too much snow for fire.

"My magic will tear you apart," I yelled at the bear. "Whatever Samir is paying you, it isn't worth your life. Run now, and I let you live."

The bear snarled, and a huffing roar barked from his mouth. I think the bastard was laughing at me.

Another ball of fire stopped that. He turned aside so it didn't catch him straight on, instead frying a painful-looking swatch of charred hair and flesh down one of his ginormous sides.

My body hurt, my feet were numb with cold, and I was burning through a lot of magic. Time to end this. Somehow. I was going to have to kill the bear.

He'd signed up for this, but I was still tired of death. No time for second-guessing or mercy. The bear clearly had no intention of showing me any.

I brought another ball of fire into my hands, making it smaller but pouring in as much will and heat as I could. I pictured more than fire, I pictured napalm, Greek fire, the worst grease fires I'd ever seen while working in commercial kitchens. I poured every memory of fire I had into the magic, honing the spell until it was a swirling purple and green sphere of death. I took every last second I could, waiting until I felt the breath of the great bear upon me, until he was only one more preternaturally quick step away.

Then I unleashed my ultimate fireball. It burned right through his side as he tried to twist again. But he was too close. He crashed into me and we fell, the snow beneath me melting away from the focused heat engulfing us both.

All my magic went right into my shields, more on instinct that by design. I closed my eyes and tried not to breathe. The bear convulsed and I shoved hard, managing to roll away from him and escape the conflagration.

A man in fatigues was watching, his gun loose in his hand and pointed at the ground, as I rose slowly to my feet. I raised a hand, gathering magic in my palm.

He dropped his gun and ran.

"Heh, normals," I muttered. At least one person here had some sense. Which was good, because I was exhausted. My body felt like it had been steamrolled by a dire bear. Funny that.

"Jade!" Ezee's voice brought me back to planet Earth and roused me from my tired fugue.

Turning, I saw him coming around the side of the church. "Okay?" I said, my voice barely above normal, but he was a shifter and heard me just fine.

"Rosie is unconscious. Something's go her bound and we think it's magic. Levi got shot, but he'll live. Come on."

"What about the other guys?"

"Levi and I killed a wolf. Harper took out a human. Nobody else down there." Ezee had blood spatter on his shirt, but from how he was moving, I didn't think it was his.

The sound of a snowmobile caused us both to jerk our heads around, but it was the one smart dude running away. I wondered if Junebug would pick him off or let him go.

I stumbled down through the storm doors to the basement. Levi waited at the bottom of the stairs, an appropriated gun in his hands. His face was paler than it should have been for a full-blood Nez Pierce, but his eyes were clear and he nodded to me as I stepped over the savaged body of a man in grey and

ANNIE BELLET

black fatigues, and made my way into the basement. Rose hadn't been locked in a bathroom but was chained with a thin silver chain to a thick wooden chair. Harper paced around her mother, clearly wanting to do something but afraid to fuck with whatever magic was holding her.

The sickly sweet scent of Samir's power washed over me in a wave and I gagged.

"Don't touch anything," I said, even though they all clearly had the picture. I pulled on more magic, digging deep. I was closer to the edge of my limits than I'd thought. Wolf appeared beside me and whined, pushing on my hip with her nose.

I stepped back and looked down at her. "Can you help?"

"Who are you... oh. Holy shitballs." Harper took a step back as Wolf let herself become visible to the rest of the group.

She circled Rose and then looked back at me with unfathomable night-sky eyes. Then her huge jaws closed on the chain. Silvery smoke puffed into the air as the chain unraveled and curled like a snake, twisting for a moment in the air as though in death throes and then dissipating.

Rose groaned and her eyelids fluttered.

"Mom, Mom," Harper rushed to her side as Wolf backed off and flopped down on the floor.

I looked at my Undying friend and whispered my thanks. Her sides were heaving as though what she had done had taxed her greatly, but watching Harper and Rose embrace was thanks enough for both of us. I went to Wolf and threaded my hand into her thick, warm fur. She felt as solid and comforting as ever.

"We should get out of here," Levi said.

"No telling when the rest will come back or where Jade's evil ex is," Ezee added, going to Rose's side and helping her stand.

She leaned heavily on Harper and Ezee, unable to stand under her own power. Pain lined her face and her eyes were puffy and red as though she'd been crying. She looked around and violently shook her head.

"Where is Max?"

"Max? He's in Washington, Mom. Remember?" Harper said, her forehead creasing.

"No, he was here. That golden-eyed monster had him here. He took him upstairs after he talked to Jade. Where is my baby? Where is my boy?" Her voice got louder, stronger, and yet rougher and more broken with each word.

I ran up the steps two at a time. The main floor of the church was empty. The pews had been pushed to the sides, blankets folded on the seats. A couple of shotguns leaned against one wall, but otherwise the place was abandoned. There was an office and another bathroom, both empty as well of anything useful. No clues about Max, no sign he'd even been here.

No sign of anything but a skeleton crew left to guard Rose. A polished chunk of obsidian resting on one of the folding card tables in the main room caught my eye. I had seen stones like it before. Without even having to summon my magic, I felt Samir's power, his presence. That rock was like the ones he'd used in the school to feed my dead family's voices to me, drawing me into his trap.

I blasted it to pieces without half a thought.

My phone, somehow undestroyed by bad landings and crushing bears, began to play the *X-Files* theme song.

Unknown caller.

With shaking fingers, I pulled it out. The screen

was cracked but I was able to flick it to answer.

Samir was on the other side, and before he spoke, I knew deep in the despairing depths of my shrinking heart exactly what he would say.

Alek called me just after Samir hung up on me. He was at the Henhouse and crazy worried. I told him to wait in the barn and stay out of sight. We took the snowmobiles and met up with Junebug, transferring the half-conscious Rose to the car. I went with Junebug, while the other three drove escort on our stolen snowmobiles.

Samir wanted Clyde's heart. He had arranged to meet us at the old rock quarry. Max's screams had confirmed he was still alive, for the moment.

It was a trap. Another one. But we were tired, injured, and I was running out of juice. Chasing down Samir and playing his games was taking too big a toll on me, but I didn't know how to stop.

Not without getting Max killed, and I wasn't willing to let that happen. I wasn't dead yet and nothing short of total annihilation was going to stop me from continuing to fight Samir.

We'd saved Rose at least. One down, one to go.

The problem was, I didn't have Clyde's heart.

I had never been so happy to see anyone as I was to see Alek. He looked tired, but was in one piece. I practically flew from the car over to him as he emerged from the barn. His big arms wrapped around me, pulling me into his warm embrace and for a long moment I let myself cling to him, breathing in his heat and his strength.

"I should never have left you," he murmured into my hair.

"Are you okay?" I asked, ignoring his stupid statement.

"No," Alek said. "But I'm here, and we'll deal with one thing at a time."

I pulled back reluctantly and looked up at him.

"What happened?"

"Long story," he said. He looked past me at the others. "For another day."

I wasn't sure we had another day, but he was right. One problem at a time.

Ezee carried Rose into the barn. Someone, I was betting Alek, had dragged the dead horses away.

It turned out that wasn't Alek, but Yosemite. The big druid walked in through a stall and nodded at us. We all gave each other the quick explanation of the previous events, from Steve's death, through my arrest, to the capture of Rose and Max. Yosemite had come and given the horses to the earth. He was done with his druid business and here to help, he said, as long as it meant not leaving the forest.

"I need Clyde's heart," I said, looking at Alek.

"You told me never to give it to you," he said. Though his ice-blue gaze was calm, his lips pressed into a tight line.

"Fuck what I said. Making the trade is the only card we have left. It's a trap, sure thing. But we need to find Samir, save Max, and end this damn thing if we can. If I can." I folded my arms over my chest, willing him to see the necessity.

"You're going to hand the heart over to Samir?" Levi asked.

"Just like that?" Ezee added.

"If it will save Max, I'll do it," Harper said, her voice tight and gravelly. "Fuck the heart. This is my brother's life."

"Samir is going to kill him anyway, Jade said so before about Rosie." Junebug stretched out a hand toward Harper.

"I'm not going to hand him the heart," I said before this could turn into a fight. Everyone was on edge and I couldn't let them turn on each other.

I took a deep breath. I had a shitty plan, but it was better than no plan.

"I'm going to pretend to hand it over. We get to the quarry with the heart, see what is what. Then I'm going to eat Clyde's heart and rain down all hell upon that bastard." Which I should have done already, I knew. I didn't want Clyde's evil inside me. I hadn't wanted his power, his memories. Universe knew what he'd done, but I was willing to bet it made a sick serial killer like Bernard Barnes look like a Bundy in diapers.

"You said it was power you didn't want," Alek

said gently in Russian. "You told me to hide it for just this reason. So you wouldn't weaken in your resolve if things got tough."

"I was an idiot," I said to him in the same language. The others were looking between us like kids watching a ping-pong match, but I shrugged off their questioning eyes.

"I've been weak," I continued. "Samir killed Steve. Right in my fucking shop. He died in my arms and I couldn't do anything. Do you see what he's done? Destroyed my friends' lives. He's probably torturing the kid while we sit here and argue. I have to stop him, Alek. I have to protect them. Save them.

"No more weakness," I added. "No more squeamishness on my part getting anyone killed. I need more power, and I'm going to take it."

"Jade," Alek said. His eyes were sad and his voice thick with resignation.

I knew I'd won. Go me.

"Take her to the heart," he said to Yosemite.

The big man looked between us and took a deep breath. "All right," he said. He rose and squeezed Ezee's shoulder. "It isn't far."

Alek and Yosemite had hidden the bag with

Clyde's heart about a ten-minute walk from the Henhouse. Two huge fir trees towered over a large rock. The stone was cracked in half, as though Paul Bunyan had split it with an axe. I knew from Alek and Yosemite's reactions that this was not how they had left it.

The bag was on the rock. The snow around us was pristine, only the bare grey stone a sign that something wasn't right, that this place had been disturbed.

I walked to the stone and picked up the bag.

It was empty.

"We can't stay here," Levi said.

"Splitting the party hasn't been working out well for us," Ezee added. He stood shoulder to shoulder with his twin. Though they looked different, Ezee with his clean-cut, professorial appearance and Levi with his tattoos, piercings, and Mohawk, their expressions were identically stubborn.

"Rose has to sleep or she won't heal. She's practically in a coma." I couldn't let them come to the quarry with me. Nobody else was allowed to get hurt, damnit. This was my fight.

"I'll take her to my grove," Yosemite said. "Nothing can approach without me knowing. We should be safe there."

"Thank you," Ezee said. He glanced at Junebug and then to Levi, his meaning clear.

Junebug sighed. "Going to try to leave me out of this fight, too, aren't you?" she said to her husband.

Levi crossed to her and slid his arms around her waist. He pressed his lips to her ear and spoke so quietly I couldn't pick up the words. Her expression grew grim, but she finally nodded.

"I'll help you with Rose," she said to Yosemite.

"You should all go with Rose," I said, knowing that even though it was futile to argue, I had to at least try. My stubborn-ass friends were going to get themselves hurt or killed. "This is a sorcerer fight."

"That he's brought shifters into," Alek said. "That alone would make it my fight. Shifters working for a sorcerer? Against their own?"

"How is the Council even putting up with this? Where are the Justices?" Levi asked. His eyes flicked to the chain around Alek's neck.

Alek bent his head and took a deep, slow breath. Then he pulled the chain out of his collar and yanked it off. The empty links fell to the barn floor.

"There are no more Justices," he said, his voice seeming to echo around the wooden walls.

"What happened in New Orleans?" I asked, breaking the stunned silence that had descended.

"There is no time to explain. I am not even sure what is happening. The world is changing, but we have more immediate trouble."

"Yeah, like saving my brother," Harper said. She clenched her fists at her sides and turned. "No more arguing. We're going with you, Jade, so suck it up and lets move."

I had nothing to say to that. They were going to go get Max with or without me, and I was their only chance of killing Samir. I couldn't fight him and my friends. I had to pick my battles. So I followed Levi out to his SUV with a heavy heart. The upside was that I was too exhausted and angry to be afraid. Only rage simmered in my veins, rage and power.

The last time I'd been out to the abandoned quarry, I'd killed a man and eaten his heart. Time for an encore.

Samir waited in the quarry. We drove as far as we could in the snow with the SUV, then Levi and I left the car and rode tandem on one of the stolen snowmobiles. The whole drive I talked with mind-Tess, both of us picking over as much about Samir as we could remember.

He loved objects, was very good at crafting them. This much was becoming painfully obvious. The stones, the wires, who knew what else? I couldn't rely on him using something like that, but I could at least try to be aware of anything he was holding or had around him. Samir had been careful with Tess as well as with me to never reveal a lot about his power. Just enough, mostly showy things, to get us interested, to prove he was like us. From there he'd played the lover and teacher, his habits and demeanor insultingly similar, as though Tess and I were interchangeable parts in his life. Toys to him.

At least Tess had known. She had played him as he played her. I had no excuse. I'd been starry-eyed, thrilled to finally find someone like me, someone who understood and wasn't afraid of my magic. My shifter family had cast me out. My human family had tried to help me, teaching me to use role-playing games to help focus and control my powers, but even they hadn't really got it. They didn't know what it felt like to have magic flowing through your blood in all its hot, elemental glory. To know that if you could just put enough into it, focus your will enough, you could change the whole freaking world and make the stars dance at your fingertips.

Samir had understood, and he had played the perfect boyfriend and mentor. Too perfect.

Tess tried to console me with the knowledge that I must have been suspicious on some level, or I never would have sought out his journals, never would have gone questing for the things he didn't tell me. I was not mollified with that thought. I should have been more suspicious. Done more. Fought him sooner instead of running and running. What had he called me? A mouse. Yeah, I'd been a fucking mouse.

And now more people were getting hurt, were getting killed because of me.

Wolf materialized by my side as I strode over the snow toward the flat plateau at the base of the quarry. The boulders blocking off the entrance carried a thick frosting of snow and the whole landscape looked glaringly white in the afternoon sun, the snow freezing into ice on top and glittering like a million diamonds. At the edge of my vision, I made out a tall dark shape standing over another dark shape. Samir and Max.

Alek, the twins, and Harper had reluctantly agreed to take the flank and let me do the approach. We paused at the boulders and I looked over at the huge white tiger to my left. He sniffed at the air, his giant head swinging from side to side as he curled his lip back, tasting as well as smelling.

"Shifters?" I whispered.

Tiger-Alek shook his head. The wind was low, but present, coming toward us from down the quarry.

Any of the mercenaries helping Samir would have had to be behind us to conceal themselves from his powerful senses. It appeared that Samir was alone with Max.

Somehow that worried me even more.

Wolf and I walked side by side, my right hand on her back, buried in her warm fur, my left clutching my D20 talisman. I let my magic flow into and around me, formless for the moment, awaiting my will. I wanted to be ready to attack or to shield, and had to hope that between Wolf and all the training I'd been doing, it would be enough. If I could draw Samir away from Max, the others might be able to get him. They'd promised to make his safety a priority, and I knew that Harper at least would keep that promise. The twins, too. Alek I was worried about, but he had a stubborn sense of duty, so I had to hope he'd see to their safety and trust me to fight my own battle.

The snow was melted away in a small area around Samir, the brown and grey ground barren. Max was prone and bent backward over a flat stone, held by magic that stung my senses even from thirty feet away. I recognized the dark bonds holding him.

Samir had definitely eaten Clyde's heart and taken his powers.

My evil ex rested his hand lightly on Max's chest. Max was still breathing, his body twitching in the bonds, his breath escaping in gasps that puffed like smoke in the cold air.

"Let him go," I said, slowing my advance. "You already have the heart." I kept my eyes on Samir but tried to pick out details with my peripheral vision. Nothing moved in the quarry.

"You did a terrible job of hiding it. Leaving it in my own bag. It was far too easy." Samir lifted a shoulder in a half-shrug and pressed down on Max's chest. Max screamed, and I heard fox-Harper snarl behind me.

I waved her back and took another step toward Samir. Something glinted at his throat. A necklace of some kind, with a smoky crystal spinning slowly on a silver chain. That worried me, too, but it gave me ideas. I was going to get rid of that necklace first, if I could separate him from it. Magic was clearly in use here, his sickly sweet power radiating from his body, centered on the spinning stone.

Tess hadn't known I could see the magic of other

sorcerer's, so perhaps Samir didn't, either. A small advantage, but I needed every single one I could get.

"Let him go," I repeated. "You want a heart? Come take mine."

Tiger-Alek roared behind me and I twisted and yelled at him to stay back. He crouched ten feet off, snarling more quietly.

"Your heart is already as good as mine," Samir said with an exaggerated sigh. "You are starting to bore me, Jade Crow. I thought you'd put up a better fight than this."

"To be fair," I muttered, "that makes two of us."

Samir laughed. I wondered that I had ever found him attractive. His face was handsome, but he was beautiful the way that a scorpion could be beautiful. When he dropped the pretense of being a feeling, non-evil person, he was as alien to me as an insect. But worse, because a scorpion would sting out of its nature. Samir did it for fun.

"You ever thought about taking up a real hobby?" I asked, moving forward another couple steps. I could make out Max's face now, his brown eyes open, his cheeks hollow and his mouth open. "Underwater basket-weaving in the Marianas

Trench? Spelunking inside a volcano?"

"I enjoy many hobbies." Samir pressed down on Max's chest and the black bonds binding him constricted. Max screamed, his voice nearly gone, more of an echo of a scream than the real thing, as though his throat was raw and his vocal cords worn away.

"Let. Him. Go." I was nearly to the open ground now. "Why are you so afraid to fight me?"

"Afraid to fight you?" Samir laughed again, but his golden eyes turned sharper and the stone at his neck started to spin more rapidly. "You think this is only about you?"

I stepped onto the open ground, finding my footing in the slick mud and pulled my magic in around me. I could blast him backward, maybe. If I hit hard enough and caught him by surprise. I just needed to move him away from Max and my friends would have a chance to get to safety.

"You aren't hurting him because of me? Really?"

"Oh, that's definitely a side benefit. You should see your face right now. You're a mess. So desperate, so tired, so sad." Samir smiled, baring his teeth. "It's nearly time to end this. The mortals are getting restless. Their time is ending, too. Like ants in a flood, they don't see it yet. Magic is rising, Jade. You could have ruled with me."

"Okay, now you are talking the crazy talk." One more step, then I'd throw the spell. Rip that necklace off, crush the stone. Whatever it was couldn't be good.

"Soon I'll take care of you. But you've still got a little fight left. Here? Now? This particular little show isn't about you."

He leapt backward, springing away and into the snow behind Max. The stone stayed, hanging in the air, spinning and spinning like a crystal dreidel.

"It has never been you I'm afraid of," Samir added. He flung his hands out and the crystal exploded.

His retreat left me, Max, and wolf alone inside the circle of bare ground.

Circle. *Fuck.*

I threw myself at Max, pulling my magic into a shield as molten power smothered us like a tidal wave. I knew within an instant that my shield wouldn't hold as the air left my lungs and my body remembered the light weight of the dire bear with sudden fondness compared to this crushing pain. Wolf threw herself onto me, her fur expanding into darkness, flowing over both of us like a blanket of night.

The pressure lifted and I could breathe. I clung to Max, to my own power, and rode out the wave as it slammed us down a final time.

The darkness enclosing me grew thin and cold. Light shone through in pinpricks then in beams until Wolf's magic turned to golden sunlight. And just like sunlight, it faded, shining with warmth and power for a golden moment, and then gone like the sun dipping behind the horizon.

"Wolf," I screamed. I cast out my hands, reaching for her. I pushed my mind out, too, hunting for the feel of her nearby. I always knew when she was here, a shadow, a presence. She was as much a part of me as my skin.

It was like fishing without a lure. My lines floated in the water, drifting, cut, useless.

Wolf was gone.

Max gasped and groaned beneath me. The rock was pulverized and we lay in a jumbled pile of gravel and mud. I dragged up the vestiges of my magic and climbed to my feet, looking for Samir.

Samir was gone as well. In the distance, I heard a snowmobile start up. Harper sprang into the circle and turned human, grabbing Max, checking him over, babbling words that hardly made sense as she told him to lie still, that he'd be okay.

"He ran," Levi said, stumbling to my side as he shifted from wolverine to human in a blink. "Alek tried to give chase but got thrown aside." He pointed to Alek's body.

I sprinted through the snow, barely conscious, hardly able to breathe.

Alek had shifted to human and he lay on his back, gasping. Alive. Relief flooded through me, taking the adrenaline with it. I collapsed to my knees and wrapped my arms around him.

Wolf was gone. Dead? I didn't know. I shoved aside the crushing fear and clung to my lover. He was alive. Max was alive.

Samir was right. I still had fight left in me. The end game was coming, I felt it. He'd attracted a lot of notice with his stunts here. While he seemed to not care, he'd always been circumspect, as most of us supernaturals were, about rousing human interest and ire. He couldn't keep doing what he was doing without attracting more notice.

I had a feeling the next time he came for me, it would end things. One way or another.

"Jade," Harper screamed, bringing me back to the present. "Help me, something is wrong with Max!"

I stumbled to my feet, looking down at Alek.

"Wind knocked out," he said. "Go, I'm fine."

Max lay where I'd left him, groaning, his face contorted in agony. I reached for my magic and saw the dark bindings still around him. It was like the unicorn all over again, only this time, I had no help from the very essence of the forest.

I tore into the twisting magic, but it was like trying to rip apart smoke with my bare hands. They dissipated and reformed, coming back like a hydra for every link that I burned.

"No," I muttered. "Don't you die on me, Max. Not today."

"I'm sorry," he said. Blood sprayed in pink foam from his lips. "Love you, Harper."

The bonds dug deeper, binding and smothering. I felt Max's life like a tiny candle, flickering beneath all that darkness. I tried to fan it with my magic, to recreate the power I'd used to save the unicorn.

There wasn't enough strength left in me, or maybe without the unicorn's own power, it would never have worked.

I failed. Max's heart stopped. One moment he was breathing beneath my hands, alive to my magic. The next, the bonds constricted and the lights went out.

Harper's wail was joined by Ezee and Levi, preternatural, haunting, and utterly broken. Hot tears rolled down my cheeks and I opened my mouth and joined my song of grief to theirs.

Harper carried Max's body to the car. She wouldn't let anyone else touch him. I rode behind Alek on a snowmobile, not wanting to face my friend. Not wanting to sit enclosed with grief and the dead body of another person I had failed to save.

Tears froze to my cheeks and despite Alek's bulk and warmth, I was chilled to the bone and all cried out by the time we reached the smoldering remains of the Henhouse. Yosemite met us there. He looked at our faces and spoke not a single word. Our expressions told the story enough.

It was slow going through the trees to his grove, and the sun started to sink in the sky. We had to abandon the snowmobiles partway into the wood as the terrain grew too rough and the brush too thick. I didn't see the grove until Yosemite parted a thick wall of brambles with the wave of one of his massive hands.

A huge ancient oak, its branches a perfect canopy and still leafy green despite the winter, shrouded a clearing. Beneath the oak, the ground was open and uncovered, no trace of snow. Tiny purple flowers bloomed as though it were summer and the air was warm. Under the tree was a small hut formed of earth and branches.

Beneath my feet I felt a heavy throb, as though the land itself here had a heartbeat. I bent and laid my fingers against the grass, pressing my magic down into the earth. A node, the confluence of magical ley lines that traced the whole of the planet. True wild magic. I'd touched ley lines before, though never tapped one. It was too dangerous. The magic within couldn't be contained for long and violently resisted attempts to channel it. I'd never felt a node this strong, not even the one that Barnes had tried to tap with his ritual last summer. It didn't surprise me that the druid had his grove here. This place was infused to the molecules with magic.

For the first time in days, I almost felt safe.

The hut was bigger on the inside than it looked. Rose was awake and Harper went to her, collapsing in her mother's lap. I hovered in the door, but stayed outside, turning away as soon as I registered that everyone within was whole and sound. I couldn't take more grief, not right now.

Instead I found a place in the flowers and knelt. I reached for Wolf again, but the void was still there. She was gone.

Alek sat behind me and pulled me back against him. We rocked there in each other's arms for a long time as the sun sank out of sight into the trees. There was nothing to say. I had lost another fight against Samir, had lost my guardian. She was one of the Undying. *Undying my ass.* Wolf had given herself to save me. Her death was another notch on the stick of my failures.

The best I could hope for was that the kind of magic Samir had thrown at us to kill her had taxed him as much as it would have taxed me. I remembered the crushing wave of power and didn't think I could have done anything so strong.

Hopefully he was exhausted.

Finally, in Alek's arms, warm for the first time that day, I fell into exhausted and fitful sleep.

We buried Max at dawn. Yosemite opened a grave in the earth and we threw flowers picked from the grove in before the earth swallowed Max forever.

No one said any words. Rose and Harper stood holding hands, fat, silent tears slowly dripping down their cheeks. Ezee and Levi and Junebug held hands as well. A united front, brought closer in grief and pain.

It didn't seem right, leaving Max in an unmarked grave. I looked around and settled on the biggest rock I could see.

"Alek," I whispered. "Can you move that?" I pointed at the stone, which was about twice the size of my head.

Alek nodded and lifted it as though were a bag of groceries. He carried it to Max's grave. I knelt and put one hand on the stone and the other on my talisman. Sleeping in Alek's arms, or perhaps sleeping on top of a huge active node, had revived my magic. I felt almost normal. Too angry to be tired anymore.

I channeled magic, going on will and instinct more than practice. The stone shifted and changed under my power, its mass converting to dark blue crystal. I anchored it into the earth, sending crystal roots out to hold it against earthquake, human intervention, or inclement weather. This stone would stay put short of someone digging it out with a backhoe.

"Thank you," Harper said to me as I finished.

I shook my head and turned, walking back to the grove. She had nothing to be thankful for. All I had done was get her brother killed. A stupid gesture at his grave? Meaningless. My magic was useless if I couldn't protect the people I loved.

I had to convince them to leave, to go into hiding. Samir had said he was getting tired of this game. Well, good. I was tired of it, too. If they hid and I offered myself up, perhaps he and I could have a final battle.

One was I fairly sure I'd lose. I needed more power. More of a plan. More knowledge. Instead, all I knew was that Samir liked objects and he liked to get hands on.

Oh, and he really wanted to fuck up and kill everyone I ever loved. Totally useless knowledge.

I waited as everyone filed back into the grove.

"We have to run," I said, though by "we" I did mean everyone but myself.

"Fuck that," Harper said. There were nods all around and grim, determined faces. Great.

"I'm going to get you all killed. This is a sorcerer problem. I've failed, okay? Don't you see? This is all my fault." My nails dug into my palms and I blinked back tears. I had to make them understand.

"Your fault?" Harper said, raising a hand to forestall Levi and Ezee, who had both opened their mouths at the same time. "You killed Steve? You kidnapped and killed my brother?"

"Because of me," I said. "If I weren't here, Samir wouldn't have come after them. He only wants to hurt all of you because of me." I paced away from them and turned back. "This is why I should have left a long time ago."

I'd chosen to stay and fight, to stop running. To live. It had felt so good to be a part of something again, to have a lover and friends and a place to belong. I'd forgotten the part where it would all be ripped horribly away from me.

"Fuck. You." Harper stalked toward me, a growl issuing from her human throat. Her green eyes flared gold for a moment and her lips curled back in a snarl.

"Let's play *It's A Wonderful Life* the Jade Crow version. So what if you'd left? Mom would be dead by now, starved and drained like a fox battery by that Barnes guy. Hell, so would Ezee. Maybe the rest of us. We weren't exactly winning that fight before you showed up."

"I could have left after that," I said weakly. "Everything bad that has happened since has been my fault, because of Samir."

"And let all the wolves die? Let Eva destroy the packs and become the Stalin version of the Alpha of Alphas? Was that Samir? I don't think so."

"Someone would have stopped her," I muttered.

"You stopped her. You threw yourself on a freaking bomb. You got shot for us. You saved my mom and Ezee. You didn't kill Max, Jade. Your evil fucking ex did. Don't you dare try to take on the blame for that. He has to pay. He has to suffer and die."

"At what cost?" I asked her.

"Any. Fucking. Cost," Harper said. She was toe to toe with me, staring into my eyes with a fire I'd never seen in her. "Samir is going to die. And the only way to kill a sorcerer is for another sorcerer to eat their heart. So stop throwing yourself a fucking pity party for shit you didn't do, and man up. We're in this together and we need you."

I wrapped my arms around her, hugging her fiercely to me.

"I love you, furball," I said. "I'm so sorry."

"I love you, too," she whispered, gripping me hard enough to bruise my ribs. "Now let's stop talking about turning tail and figure out how we destroy that motherfucker."

We spent the morning brainstorming in the grove. By midday, we were all tired of talking in circles, trying to decide how to get Samir to hold still long enough to really fight him. It seemed we would have to wait for him to come to us. Yosemite had the most strength here in the grove and he would be able to sense anyone approaching, so it seemed like a good spot to make our stand.

We needed supplies. It was dangerous to leave, but neither the druid nor I could conjure food, weapons, ammo, or blankets. The hut had the bare bones of things, some dried food and a couple blankets, but nothing that could last days and support eight people.

Alek and I, and the twins, decided to hike out. The twins would go for weapons. Levi had another rifle stashed at his shop, and Ezee said he'd put a call in to the wolf pack, certain they could help hook him up. Freyda hadn't left town, which worried me. I hoped my message to Sheriff Lee had gotten through.

The day was grey and dim outside the magical grove. Occasional snow spit from the sky, more ice than flakes. We reached the barn and split up, Alek and I taking his truck, Levi and Ezee taking snowmobiles.

"Any sign of trouble, you GTFO," I warned them.

"No shit, Sherlock," Levi said with a half-assed grin.

"Do you smell smoke?" Alek asked, turning his face into the wind.

"I smell the burned building over there," I said, though my nose was too numb to smell much of anything. I kept my eyes off the wrecked heap of the Henhouse. So many happy hours spent inside those walls. It was just a burned-out shell now, hollow and broken.

"No," Ezee said, sniffing also. "I smell smoke. Fresh smoke." He looked around and then pointed. "There."

In the distance, a huge black cloud hung in the air. It looked like storm clouds, but the season was wrong for that kind of storm, and the cloud was too black, too thick. Too low.

"That's Wylde," I said softly, giving voice to what we were all probably thinking. "That's the direction of town."

Alek drove his truck at not quite ludicrous speed. I'd made Levi and Ezee stick to the plan. Alek and I would investigate the smoke; they would go get weapons and stuff.

Wylde was burning. Smoke billowed down the main street as we drove past the gas station and courthouse.

My shop was at the heart of the conflagration. Two fire engines were trying to stem the damage, but the water seemed to be making the fire angrier. Every cop car in the county, plus two state patrol vehicles, created a blockade of the main strip. Police in hospital masks and heavy jackets were trying to wave back the mass of onlookers as people desperately jostled for both a view and to stay away from the worst of the radiating heat.

Alek pulled up a block away, and I was out of the truck before it had fully stopped moving. I ran toward the fire, reaching out with my magic, already sensing Samir's power somehow involved. The fire reacted to my own power by flaring up, bright orange flames roaring into the sky. My whole building was a raging inferno, but flames were already jumping further along, catching the roofs of the buildings next door.

Apparently Samir was done with subtle. He was trying to burn down the entire town.

"Jade!" Rachel Lee ran toward me, waving her arms.

"What happened?" I yelled over the noise of shouting people, crackling and roaring fire, and the scream of more sirens as another fire engine came up from the other side.

"It won't stop burning," she yelled back. "Went up half an hour ago. Fire chief says he's never seen the like."

"It's magic," I said. It wasn't going to stop. There

was something fueling it. I didn't think Samir would stand at the center of such a blaze, if he were even capable of it.

He likes objects. Making things, mind-Tess whispered.

I closed my eyes and pushed my magic back at the building, forming it like a probe. I ignored the renewed pulse of the fire, the answering song of Samir's sickly sweet power, and tried to feel for a catalyst. There, in my shop. That was the center, a knot of magic holding the fire in its grasp, fueling it.

I was too far away to undo the knot, to destroy whatever was anchoring the spell.

Pulling off my jacket, I looked over at Alek. He shook his head with a warning, an unhappy look on his face.

"Hold this," I said. I stripped out of my shirt next, then my jeans, panties, socks, and shoes.

"Jade," Alek said softly as he took my clothes from me. The wind and noise stole the sound of my name from his lips, but I made out the word.

"What are you doing?" Rachel yelled as I started walking, totally naked, straight at the fire.

"It won't stop without help," I yelled back at her.

"Tell them to let me through."

Rachel, to her credit, didn't argue, just started shouting at the firemen to let me through.

Not that they listened. To their eyes, a naked Native American woman wearing only a necklace was walking right at a million alarm fire. Men in heavy gear tried to grab me.

The time for subtlety was past. I used magic to more or less gently shove them aside. The fire brought sweat to my face, whispering of the heat to come as I neared the building. I pulled my magic around me. I'd survived a damned bomb. I could manage a little fire. Fire and me had always seemed to have an understanding.

I had Haruki's power inside me, as well. Fire had been a favorite of his. He knew its ways, knew glyphs to summon it, and to quell it. I painted myself with glyphs of pure magic, covering my skin in a second glittering shield as purple fire formed its own marks along my body.

Then I stepped into the blaze. My eyes watered and I didn't want to risk breathing, so my lungs felt tight and empty.

This won't kill me, I told myself. I didn't need to

breathe. The fire left my skin alone. It felt as though I'd walked into a dry sauna, oppressive but not unbearable. I walked over the remains of my life here, eyes mostly closed against the thick smoke. I moved by instinct and memory, not sight.

This store had been my home, my sanctuary, for nearly six years. Every miniature I'd painted here, every comic I'd bought and sold, every dragon my friends and I had slain together. All the happiness I'd had in decades was in flames, burning away as though it had never mattered.

But it had. I used those memories to strengthen my shield. Samir was trying to take everything from me, but I still had my family. Their love. The laughter and tears and hopes that we had all shared.

I still had everything that this store represented.

This was still my town, and I wasn't going to roll over and let it burn. I reached the center of the fire and pressed my magic out, feeling for the thing I'd sensed from outside.

The catalyst was not a rock. A snake that looked to be formed of lava and hellfire uncoiled from the center of the blaze, its mouth open in a silent hiss. Or perhaps not so silent, but I couldn't hear anything over the crackle and roar of the flames in my ears.

I dodged as it struck and my hip slammed into a fallen beam. Part of the upstairs had collapsed down, the subflooring giving way as the fire ate it. Rolling while holding tightly to the glyph shield keeping me safe from the flames, I lashed out with my feet, slamming into a coil of the firesnake.

It felt like I kicked a block of steel. Pain jarred up my legs and I skidded back, ash and smoke swirling up around me, blocking what little vision I had.

The snake struck again, this time catching my left arm. Its molten teeth bit through my shield. Pain so hot it became cold again radiated into my arm and the smell of cooked meat filled my nostrils. I rammed a bolt of pure force into the snake's head from point-blank range with my right hand, knocking it back and away from me.

My left arm hung useless and numb. I was glad for the numb. That jolt of pain had nearly knocked me out. I renewed my shield as I scrambled back, my smoke-teared eyes hunting for the snake. I missed Wolf more than ever as I tried to regain my feet and get my back up against something more solid than burning wood.

I couldn't fight fire with fire. I had to stop just reacting.

Dragons, I thought. *What if this were a red dragon?*

We'd have boned up on ice spells, ice enchantments, and fire-protection gear. That was what a good adventurer would have done.

Tess had told me my gift, my specialty in sorcery was elemental magic. It was freaking winter outside this raging inferno. There was snow everywhere and freezing air.

I reached for it, envisioning myself like the center of a black hole, sucking in as much air as I could. The fire flared and grew as I pulled oxygen into it, but I held on, focusing on the cold. Focusing on how it had felt to fly through the air, tears freezing to my cheeks as I raced to try and save Rose and Junebug.

Then I visualized deeper. Glaciers. Swirling blizzards. Dry ice. Cold so strong that blood would freeze in the veins of living things. I set my will on that cold, pushed my magic into ice around me.

The snake struck again, twisting and lashing out as I hit it with the strongest cold area of effect spell I could muster. Ice and snow blasted out from my body, the air freezing instantly. Ice formed and encased the snake, catching it in a deadly embrace.

More of the second floor collapsed under the weight of flame and magic. I'd be buried before I killed the damn snake at this rate. Unless I could slow down time.

I reached for Tess's magic then, slowing time around the snake and I. Holding three spells at once made my head spin and my stomach turn to cheese. My knees gave out and I fell forward, but I clung to the magic, pouring everything I had into the ice.

The snake's body hardened and drew dark. Embers flared and died in the pits of its eyes.

Then the fire died, as though it had never been. I let go of all of my spells and knelt, hands and knees on the floor, gasping in cold, smoky air. The floor was freezing, rimed with frost and no more flames licked at the building.

Voices roused me from my exhausted slump. Shouting from outside.

I made myself stand and walk toward the street. The entry was mostly crushed, the building half collapsed, but I clambered over fallen beams and charred wall. Firemen stood around, some pointing, many talking at once, as I strode out of the building toward Alek.

"Jade." Rachel rushed at me, grabbing a blanket from a surprised fireman and throwing it around me.

I winced as the cloth hit my injured arm. The numbness was wearing off and it felt like my flesh was still on fire.

Alek reached us a moment later, his glare driving back the two men trying to approach. People were yelling a lot of things, but compared to the roar of the fire, it was almost eerily quiet.

I looked back at my building. The blaze was completely out. Smoke still hung above the building, but nothing seemed to burn or smolder within. Score one for me, I guess.

I wanted to curl up in a ball and sleep for a thousand years, but I pulled the blanket around myself and tried on a smile for Alek's sake.

"I'm okay," I lied. My shop was gone. The picture that Ji-hoon had drawn for me, the last remnant of the people I'd lost, was gone as well. It was the only thing I'd truly prized, the one possession I'd carried through the decades. I'd just performed a crazy amount of magic, further weakening myself. And I'd done it in front of a hundred people, some of whom were definitely normals. Added to my aching arm, it all summed up to very not okay.

"Let's get you to the truck before anyone starts asking what happened," Alek said. He pushed my clothes into Rachel's arms and swept me up like a child.

I was almost used to him carrying me at this point. It was sort of our thing. I perform big magic, Alek sweeps me off my feet when I'm too tired to stay on them. I was supposed to protest, but I was too fucking tired.

Nobody tried to stop us. Awe and disbelief painted the faces around us as Alek strode back to the truck.

Detective Hattie Wise and Agent Salazar waited by the truck, unhappy looks on their faces.

"You are causing a lot of trouble," Hattie said.

"I didn't start the damn fire," I said as Alek growled at her to get out of his way.

"This is getting national media attention," Salazar said. His lips were pressed into a tight line and his forehead creased with worry marks. They both looked like they'd aged a decade since I'd seen them.

"That's your problem," I said. "Remember? You can't stop a sorcerer. So get out of my way. Unless you want to arrest me for putting out a fire."

Hattie nodded slowly. Salazar looked like he wanted to protest, but she laid a hand on his arm and pulled him back.

Alek set me down on the bench seat. Rachel laid my clothes in my lap.

"Get the wolves out," I told her. "Get away from here. This might get worse." I could only hope that Samir would come for us in the woods and stop fucking up my town. My shop was gone. There was nothing left for him here.

"Good luck, Jade," she said, her dark eyes solemn. "And thank you."

I didn't know what she was thanking me for. Maybe putting out the fire. It was hard to tell and I was too tired to care. I clutched the blanket around myself and passed out even as Alek started the engine.

The bird hits the glazed windowpane with a sickening thud. Tess runs out the door, ignoring the call of her grandmother to stop, to leave it be.

The bird is dead. Its neck is twisted and Tess cries. Something strange and cold unfurls within her, swirling through her mind. She begs God to let the bird live again, to turn it away from the window.

The world swirls around her. The cabin looks as though it is no thicker than her paper dolls, an image she could push over with the shove of one of her tiny hands.

"NO!" Gran's voice cuts through the chill and the world stops its slow spin.

"Heal him," Tess says, pushing out her lower lip. "I wanted to fix it. To stop the bird from hitting the window."

"You cannot do this, honey-child. Ever. God wills what happens and what does not." Gran takes the bird from Tess's hands. "We'll give him a proper burial."

Later, sitting at the hearth and watching Gran spin in the waning light, Tess gets the courage to ask.

"What was happening? I felt all cold, and the world started to spin and spin."

"It's your gift. Like your mama before you. You have a feel for time, for the way the world and stars and all the heavens move." Gran sighs and stills the drop spindle, setting it in her lap.

Tess stays quiet. Gran never talks about Tess's mama. Not ever.

"She had the sight, which has passed you by, I pray to Jesus. Your mama saw the devil coming and she tried to change the future. Look at me, child. No one can change the future. Only God can stand up to the devil. But my baby tried."

Gran's eyes left Tess's face and focused on something Tess couldn't see, a distance she sensed but did not understand.

"She gave her life to you," Gran said after a long, long silence that left Tess fidgeting and wondering if her Gran had fallen asleep with her eyes open. "Like Jesus dying for us, she tried to give her life to you, to die for your sins."

"I'm a good girl," Tess said, distressed. She said her prayers every night. She walked all the way to church twice a week, and she always asked God to forgive her when she had bad thoughts about the mean Camberly boys.

"You are," Gran agreed. "But you must never turn back time. Your mama tried it, the night she died. I can't say for sure if she managed, but I've never known a woman able to survive what she did. A baby, neither."

"How did she die?" Tess whispered. She had an idea, a vague memory that was impossible. A beautiful woman with long brown hair leaning over her, whispering in a language Tess did not understand. Telling her to eat, to remember, to live.

Telling her to fight the devil.

"She gave her life for yours," Gran said. Her grey braids bobbed as she shook her head. "That's enough woolgathering. Go wash your hands and say your prayers."

Tess knelt by her bed. She closed her eyes and tried to remember the beautiful woman.

Words tumbled from her lips, but they weren't her usual prayers.

"Lucifer has golden eyes. The man comes, mama. The devil is coming to burn and burn us all. The devil is going to end the world. Lucifer will wake the dragon."

I awoke with strange words and memories on my lips, shaking myself out of Tess's memory, or her dreams. It was hard to tell them apart. Tess stayed silent in my mind, her ghost weeping softly at the edge of my consciousness. She was terrified.

I didn't blame her. I was in the barn, up in the loft. Alek's warm body was pressed against my back. Light filtered in through the bullet holes. It was still daylight.

"Hey," I said, not sure if he was awake.

He was. "You want water or clothes first?" he asked.

"Water," I said. My mouth tasted of ash and

blood.

My left arm was still pink and raw, but healing. I splashed water over it after taking a deep drink. Minimal pain, just the sting, no worse than a papercut but less annoying. My fingers flexed fine. I'd live.

"What happened in the fire?" Alek said as he handed me my clothing.

"Some kind of magical snake thing. Like a Salamander without legs, I guess. Lava snake? Who knows. The important thing is that it tried to eat me and I kicked its ass."

I was filthy, covered in ash and soot. I wondered if the hose still worked but was too tired to climb down and find out. It was probably frozen sold anyway. All I'd do would be to make myself wet, dirty, and cold. So I sucked it up and pulled on my clothing. At least it was dry, warm, and less dirty than my skin.

My hair was unraveling from its braid. I did what I could with it, twisting it into a thick knot at the base of my neck. I was halfway tempted to tell Alek to chop it all off, but it could be saved with a hot shower and conditioner. A few hours with a brush and a lot of patience wouldn't have hurt, either. I had none of the above, but I still had my vanity. I loved my hair. It was staying, itchy and annoying though it was at the moment.

"Where are Ezee and Levi?" I asked, looking around. "How long was I out?"

"A couple of hours. They are getting supplies. It'll be dark soon. We're going to stay here for the night and head to the grove at first light."

"Do the others know? If we don't come back, they might come looking for us." I knew that Harper would. She was stubborn that way. Given Ezee and Yosemite's relationship, there was a good chance he'd go with her. Then we'd be all split up again, ripe for picking off. I didn't like that idea at all.

"Yes. Ezee called Harper. Cell phones are magical, aren't they?" Alek smiled gently at me.

I felt my jeans pocket. My phone was missing. "Don't suppose you know where mine is?" I asked.

"Dead somewhere along the way," Alek said. "That's my guess. It wasn't on you or in the clothes you handed me."

"Damn. Not again." My life was hell on phones. And clothing, for that matter. At least this time I'd saved my shirt, and Harper's jacket.

Alek raised his head, listening, his body tense. He relaxed quickly as the sound of a car crunching on ice and gravel reached my less sensitive ears.

"Twins?" I asked, though his posture already told me he recognized the vehicle.

I wrapped my hand around my talisman just in case. It had survived the fire just fine, but I kind of figured it would. The D20 was as much a part of me as Wolf.

Shit. As Wolf had been. I sucked in a deep breath to quell my grief. For a moment I'd forgotten.

"Hey," Levi called out.

"Up here," Alek called down to him.

They had backpacks full of granola bars, jerky, and dried fruit. We ate a quick meal, nobody talking much for a while as the sun faded away. I hated winter. It got dark so early and it felt like the sun took its sweet time rising, too, like it was too cold to get up and it just hung around considering not making the effort.

"Town didn't burn, I heard," Ezee said after a while. "Thanks to a crazy naked woman."

I gave them the cliff-notes version.

"Shit, lady." Levi grinned at me, his teeth white in

the growing gloom, his face in shadow, only his piercings catching the light and glinting silver.

"I know I can't talk Harper out of her revenge," I said, burrowing into one of the sleeping bags and leaning back against Alek. "But you two should take Rose and Junebug and get the hell out of here. This is my fight."

"Fuck that," they said in unison.

"Samir came here, burned our town, killed our friends, and is trying to destroy the rest of our friends. We aren't abandoning you," Levi said.

"I'd be insulted you are even asking us to, but I know your heart is in the right place. Stupid, but in the right place." Ezee pulled a blanket around his shoulders and moved a mound of hay to help pillow his head.

"I don't know if I can win," I murmured. I barely said the words aloud, but my friends had preternatural hearing, so it didn't matter.

Alek's arms tightened around me and he nuzzled my ear.

"You are the strongest person I've ever met," he said. "And you are not alone."

"Damn straight," Levi said.

"Correct, but never straight," Ezee added. I heard the smile in his voice even as the light faded too much for me to make out his features. It was an old joke among us.

"I feel like we're always behind. I can't pin Samir down. I don't even know what his real game is, what he really wants. He could have killed me by now." At least, I was pretty sure he could have. Maybe Wolf had been more of a deterrent than I thought, but it seemed like Samir was up to more than just toying with me. That, or I truly didn't comprehend the depths of his evil. Little from column A, little from column B?

"It's obvious what game he's playing," Levi said with a snort. "*Human Occupied Landfill*, live action version."

"What?" I said. I hadn't thought about that obscure game in a long time. I'd had a copy in the game store, but mostly as a novelty item.

"Think about it," Ezee said. "How do you start a live-action game of *HoL*?"

"Set a couch on fire in someone's basement?" I tried to think, remembering something along those lines from the back of the book.

"Exactly." Levi chuckled.

"If we're playing *HoL*," I said. "I guess you all took the 'running blindly into eternal damnation because you think you can win' skill, eh?"

"I think we all took that skill at char gen," Ezee said.

"Except Alek," Levi added. "He took the 'make sharp things go through soft things that scream and bleed' skill."

I managed a laugh at that as Alek nuzzled my cheek with a soft chuckle. Laughing felt good, a little painful, but cleansing.

"I like this skill," Alek said.

He was right, I wasn't alone. I was loved and surrounded by those I loved.

That's what terrified me. I had so much to lose. And I didn't want to lose anymore.

There had to be a way to protect them all. I closed my eyes, but it was a long time before I slept again. Samir would come at me again. He would finish me himself, I was certain of that. He was hands on, he'd want to see the life leave my eyes, watch me die as he bit into my heart and stole my soul. Watch the pain in my face as he destroyed everyone I loved, as he broke me before the end.

He would come to me.

I had to be ready. So I spent most of the night taking a tour of the memories in my head. Thinking about power, about magic, and ley lines, and how to save the people I loved.

When dawn came, I was tired, but determined. And I had a terrible, terrible plan.

We arrived at the grove to find that Freyda and the Wylde wolf pack had beat us there sometime in the night. At a glance, the Alpha of Alphas didn't look like much. She was tall and lean, with pale skin and wheat-colored hair. Freckles dotted her nose, giving her a younger, cuter appearance that almost mocked the worry line in her forehead and the deep knowledge in her blue eyes. She was holding the wolf pack together, and had beaten all challengers to her role. Underestimating Freyda was not something that anyone did twice.

"Not what I had in mind when I told the Sherriff to tell you to get out of town and get to safety," I said after we exchanged cautious greetings.

"You think we would run? There are strange wolves here, invading my territory without asking for passage. A man who smells of death and old blood leads them. He tried to hire some of my people." She spit into the flowers, then glanced at Yosemite where the big druid lurked near the hut and inclined her head in apology.

"As though we would fight against the woman who saved us all," she continued.

"Jade thinks everyone should run away and let her fight Samir all alone," Harper said with an exaggerated eye-roll.

I glared at Harper and sighed. I was done fighting with everyone over who could stand with me. Freyda had been around a long time. She wasn't stupid. I hoped she would realize when enough was enough and vanish when the time came.

"You may stay," I said, pretending it was my decision. I could cling to the illusion of choice and control, right? "But the sorcerer is mine. I'm the only one who can kill him. If you want to keep the mercenaries he brought with him off my back, I'd appreciate it. I won't interfere with that."

Freyda looked me over and gave a small shake of her head. I could only imagine how I appeared. Dressed all in black, filthy from the fire, my black hair tangled in a halo around my probably exhausted-looking face. From her expression, she didn't think I could kill a flea, much less Samir, but she had the intelligence, or at least the grace to not say so.

We worked out that the wolves would set up in the forest around the grove. They would be the early warning system and try to pick off Samir's men before too many reached us. Working as a pack, we hoped they could drive Samir and his people toward the grove. Yosemite was strongest here, and the thick brambles would limit the effectiveness of guns, hopefully edging the fight into melee range where the shifters and I could have a better chance of engaging the foe.

It wasn't much of a plan, but when you break eggs, you have to make omelets.

After that, it was a waiting game.

Know something else that druid hovels don't come with? Showers.

I heated water over a propane camp stove and ran

a washcloth over my face and neck. The tan cloth turned instantly black, as did the water as soon as I dunked it again.

"Hey," I said to Rose as I gave up on cleanliness. "You feeling okay?"

"I'm healing," she said. Her expression was grim and lined with grief. "As for the rest, well. Max isn't the first baby I've lost. It don't get easier."

I shivered at the hollow pain in her voice. "I'm sorry, Rosie," I said softly.

"Don't start that again," she said, looking at me with fever-bright eyes. "You just promise to keep my Azalea safe. And you kill that devil who took my Max from us."

Devil. Her use of that word echoed Tess's dream memory and ran a different kind of shiver down my spine.

"I promise," I said, meeting her gaze without flinching. "I am going to keep you all safe. Nobody else dies. Not on my watch."

With that said, I left the hut and went to find the druid.

Yosemite was at the edge of the grove, watching me approach as though he'd been waiting for me. Knowing the unfathomable ways of druids, he probably had been.

"Iollan," I said, using his given name instead of his nickname. I continued in old Irish, so that Harper, Ezee, and Levi, who were all sacked out on blankets on the other side of the clearing wouldn't be able to understand us if they overheard.

"That tree teleportation thing you did when we were fighting the Fomorians," I said. "Do you have to use trees? Could you teleport more than one person at a time?" We'd leapt into a tree portal, voluntarily and with haste. I had something else in mind this time.

He was silent a long time, his eyes fixed on my face as though it were a book he could read. Then he sighed and ran a hand through his thick red curls.

"I would say it is not possible, but we are in my grove. Here, many things might be possible."

"Because we are on the biggest node I've ever felt?" I asked, curious if he could feel it, could maybe even tap its power.

"Partially. There is a reason the Eldertree grows

here," he said, gesturing at the huge oak. "You want me to take people away from here?"

"Yes," I said simply. "When the fighting reaches us, when Samir shows up, I want you to get everyone out. Everyone," I repeated. "Except me."

Yosemite turned away and ran is fingers along a blackberry cane, tracing lines and thorns. The cane went from winter brown to summer green as I watched, then faded again back to dull, dormant.

"This is a hard thing you ask."

"I cannot watch them die," I said softly, glancing back to where my friends rested. "I need to be able to fight Samir without worrying. This is not their battle anymore. Please, Iollan. Please help me."

"Will they forgive me?" he asked, more to himself than to me. "Will he?"

I had no answer for him. I knew he and Ezee had a troubled relationship. Ezee had described it as a bird loving a fish once, but they'd grown closer over the last month. Turmoil does that, I suppose. Some people it rips apart. Others, it binds together, paring us down to our core values and desires, showing us just how damned important the ones we love are, how important that love is all by itself.

I was counting on his love for my friend. Counting on his own desire to keep them from dying, using it to get my way. I would have felt worse about manipulating the druid like this, but I needed to save my friends.

Harper wanted her vengeance, but she couldn't have it. It would only get her killed. I wasn't sure I could defeat Samir, but I'd hatched a plan.

"Do you have a plan?" Yosemite asked, almost as if reading my mind.

I looked up at him. He'd stepped back toward me and I'd forgotten how huge he was. He had a good six inches on Alek, who had a nearly a foot on me. For a moment Yosemite seemed as old and solid as the oak above us.

"I do," I said. "I need to know they are safe, or I won't be able to do what is necessary."

"Does your plan involve destroying my grove?" A dark glint of humor lurked in his eyes and the corners of his mouth twitched beneath his beard.

Maybe he could read my mind. Damnit.

"Possibly," I said. I didn't really know. It had a good chance of it though. What I planned wasn't subtle.

"Will you survive?"

"Samir won't," I said with more conviction than I felt. That was all the answer to Yosemite's question I was planning on giving.

"If you do, you'll have your hands full apologizing," he said, the smile gone.

"I'll burn that bridge when I come to it," I muttered. Alek would forgive me. Eventually.

"All right, Jade Crow. I give you my oath. When the fighting starts, I will take them away." He sighed heavily and shook his head. "What about the wolves?"

I repressed my feelings of triumph. This was not something to celebrate, but just knowing that I had Yosemite helping me, that my friends had a chance to escape and live, lifted a weight from my shoulders, unbending my spine.

"Freyda isn't an idiot," I said. "She'll do what she must out there against the other shifters. If it gets too dangerous, she'll pull back the pack." That I was sure of, more or less. She was a survivor, and her skin in this game was thin. She loved Wylde and felt duty-bound as the Alpha of Alphas, but she wouldn't risk her pack on a suicide mission. She was happy enough

HEARTACHE

to leave Samir and the true war to me.

If only my own damn friends were that pragmatic. Rushing into certain doom because they thought they could win was definitely a feat those loveable bastards all had in common, the twins were right about that.

"How quickly can you get them away?"

He rubbed his beard in a gesture that mimicked Ezee's usual joking one, looking almost professorial himself.

"Not quickly. I will have to use the earth to transport them away. We will not get very far, and I will need them clustered. Especially if they are unwilling."

"Oh, they'll be unwilling," I said.

"Aye." Yosemite gave me a sardonic look. I supposed I was being Captain Obvious again.

"So you'll have to wait and do it when they are distracted. That'll be more dangerous." I didn't like it, but it was the best plan we had. "How far can you get them?"

"A couple miles. I have a destination in mind. That will be almost equally dangerous. If I lose my grip on anyone, they could be lost and end up who knows where, if the earth spit them back out at all."

Great. So if this went wrong, my friends could be lost in time and space. Awesomesauce.

"I know it isn't the best plan. But staying here and watching them die while I'm too distracted to save them is worse. Just… do what you can." By which, I meant "save them all" but I decided to stop saying the obvious while I was ahead. He'd agreed to try and given me his oath. That was all I needed.

Yosemite moved away from me and I took the hint, walking back into the grove. I sank down on the warm bed of flowers and lay back. Summoning my magic, I gently probed the node. Raw power sang beneath me, as vast and unknowable as the ocean.

Yep, terrible plan. But it was the only one I had.

I guessed I had taken the same damn feat at char gen. Go me.

Alek found me laying there and sprawled beside me. Everyone else was still curled up, though Levi and Junebug were talking softly. The air had an expectant quality, though the day felt slow and lazy in the artificial warmth of the grove.

"What are you planning?" Alek said to me in Russian. He clearly didn't want anyone understanding our conversation.

"To kill Samir," I said, evading his question as best I could.

"You are too calm," he said. His ice-blue eyes caught my gaze and held it, assessing.

"I could freak out more," I offered. "But I'm tired and I think I should save my energy."

"Wolf is gone?" he asked after a moment of silence stretched between us.

I closed my eyes at the pain those words roused in me and nodded.

"Whatever she did, trying to stop Samir's magic, it killed her."

"She is Undying. They cannot die. By definition." Alek shook his head.

"More by legend," I said. "Before, all my life, I could sense her presence. Even when she wasn't nearby or visible, I knew she was there. Like my shadow. Not always visible, but when conditions are right, it is always following. Now? Nothing. I feel like a ship whose anchor has been cut."

"You are not without harbor," he said, his voice low and soothing.

I crawled into his arms, burying my head into his chest. He'd forgive me when Yosemite took them away, I was sure of it.

But only if I lived. I was equally sure that Alek would never forgive me for dying.

"I'm going to try," I murmured into his chest. "I'm going to win. No one else is going to die because of me."

"I know," he said. "You will do what you must, kitten. No one will die because of you. Steve, Peggy, Max, they weren't your fault."

"Close enough," I muttered. "No one else. No one." Those words were my litany, my new compass point in the storm.

"We cannot take responsibility for the actions of others," Alek said. "Only our own."

"What happened in New Orleans?" I asked him, wanting to change the subject before he coaxed me into spilling my plan and ruining the surprise.

His body stiffened and he rubbed his nose in my hair, his arms tightening around me.

"It is a long story," he said after a moment. "The

Justices have been dissolved. Our powers and feather of office stripped from us. The Council has gone silent, for the most part."

"For the most part?" I leaned back and looked up at him.

His blue eyes were shadowed and staring into the middle distance.

"I think one of the Council tried to kill me," he said. "Carlos and…" he trailed off and pressed his lips together. "Carlos and I stopped them."

"Is Carlos okay?"

"He'll live," Alek said grimly. "Barely survived, but he made the right choice when the time came. I do not know what will come of this. I do not think I understand the world anymore."

"Was it because of Eva?" I thought about the wolf Justice who had tried to become Alpha of Alphas, who had tried to destroy the Peace and broken all her vows as Justice.

"I believe she was more of a symptom than the disease," Alek said.

I studied his face. I could only imagine how hurt he must feel about it all, how lost. Over half a year ago when I'd met him, he had been so sure of right and wrong, the perfect judge, jury, and executioner.

"What are you thinking about?"

"How full of vim and vigor you were when we met."

"As opposed to the old man I am now?" he said, smiling a little.

"More like how you waltzed into my shop and accused me of murder. And here we are, waiting for a guy to show up so I can murder the hell out of him." I nipped his chin, wanting him to keep smiling. I wanted to remember him like this, big and strong and curled around me with eyes full of love. I wanted to take his belief in me and forge it into invincible armor.

"Life is strange," he said. "I never thought I would have a mate. I have always been a Justice, since I was barely more than a cub. It was who I am."

"It *is* who you are. Remember what you told me about balance? You have justice in your soul, Aleksei Kirov. You can't help but do what you think is best for everyone around you. It's annoying, but kind of endearing, too."

"Only kind of endearing?" He kissed me, pulling me into an embrace so tight that I had to protest lest

I lose a rib.

It almost worried me how affectionate he was being. How he clung to me like I was his anchor in a storm. It almost felt like he knew I was going to try and send him away. As though he knew what I was planning. I shoved all that aside. This was potentially our last day together. I couldn't let doubt or fear stop me. I loved this man, every damn inch and frustrating flaw. Every perfect muscle and stubborn devoted molecule of him.

He was right. He was my mate. He was mine, damnit, just as I belonged in a strange way to him. Maybe I'd always known it, since those first uncomfortable moments in my store where I was both attracted and appalled by him.

He might never forgive me, but I would keep him safe. I was going to protect my own. No more running for me. No more letting people die because I flinched at doing the hard things I needed to do. No more weakness.

"I love you," I murmured to him. Then his lips came down over mine and we forgot we weren't alone for a while. If anyone noticed us curled among the flowers, they were too smart to say a word.

It was near dusk, the sun a bloody blur behind flat grey clouds, when the forest fell utterly silent. Winter wasn't a loud season in the woods, but the branches still rustled, a few birds still flitted here and there. The woods had a living, breathing quality to them, a background noise to filled even my duller senses.

Quiet could only mean one thing. Trouble. *Something wicked this way comes,* mind-Tess whispered to me.

Yosemite rose to his feet and around my friends shifted form. Rose emerged from the hut as a fox and paced up to be with her daughter, red and grey next to each other.

I admit, it felt somewhat comforting to have a twelve-foot tiger at my side. He was huge and solid and I loved Alek all the more in that moment as eerie silence descended upon our ragtag band of wannabe warriors.

The last stand.

I met Yosemite's eyes as I let my magic flow into me. "What is it?"

"Something is coming, but I can't track it, or perhaps them? It feels like they are all around us." The big druid turned slowly in a circle, his eyes hunting the shadows beyond the grove.

"What about Freyda? Can you sense her?" I wanted to tell him to do it now, to get everyone out right damn now, but I couldn't. Not yet. He couldn't get them far enough that they would be out of the fight, not for certain. I knew my bullheaded friends would turn around and charge right back to try and help me. Even in this terrain, in winter, a few miles wouldn't slow down a giant Siberian tiger, not for long.

"I can't sense the wolves. They are too far out."

The staccato burst of gunfire punctuated his statement and we all stiffened, turning toward the noise.

Owl-Junebug lifted off from her perch on a lower branch of the oak.

"Stop," I called to her but she ignored me, soaring up into the gloom.

Wolverine-Levi whined low in his throat, clearly no more happy about her decision to go take a look than I had been. The thick hair on his back stood up and his huge claws dug into the earth as he watched her fly away.

"Back up," I said to my friends. "Closer to the tree. It can guard our backs."

Alek swung his head toward me, his tiger eyes suspicious. I wondered if he still had the power to detect lies. I wasn't outright lying, as impure as my motives were. The great oak would guard our backs. It was also help group everyone together so that when Samir showed and the fighting started for us, Yosemite could get them out.

Except Junebug, who spiraled above us, scouting. I hoped she had enough sense to stay out of fight if she was beyond Yosemite's reach. She wasn't much of a fighter in her animal shape, built more for silent speed and grace than brawn.

Something huge moved just beyond the grove, a white shadow in the dark brambles.

Junebug screamed a warning, banking to the south. Another crack of gunfire snapped through the air and she swung sideways, then plummeted into the trees below.

A giant white bear smashed into the brambles, bursting through and into the grove as wolverine-Levi screamed challenge and ran in the direction his wife had fallen.

I couldn't let him get far. Things were happening too quickly.

"Iollan," I yelled. "Oath!"

I sent a bolt of pure force into the face of the giant bear, forcing it to slow its charge as it twisted aside. Its teeth were as long as my arm, its mouth opened wide enough to swallow half my torso and not even have to burp. This beast made the bear I'd defeated before look like a child's toy, cuddly and small.

Yosemite was chanting, green light spilling from the ancient oak tree. Tendrils of it started to wrap around my friends, pulling them backward.

Tiger-Alek snarled and broke free of the druid's grasp.

"No," I cried out, sending more magic into the bear. Its hide started to smolder as raw fire burned into it. I wasn't pulling punches. The finale of this wouldn't depend just on my own power, so I wasn't holding reserves. I had to keep my friends clear of this thing long enough for Yosemite to get them out.

Tiger-Alek hesitated as a glowing ball flew into the clearing, landing nearly at my feet. The sickly sweet smell of Samir's magic flowed over me in a wave.

I grabbed at the glowing stone, trying to fling it away with magic.

Too late. Alek threw himself at me, carrying me beyond the stone.

It burst like a grenade, molten bits of pain lancing through my legs. Tiger-Alek screamed above me, roaring. His blood showered me as molten stone ripped straight through his chest, but he rolled before he crushed my body beneath his.

I struggled to my feet, saying his name over and over. To my right, Ezee and Levi had engaged the bear, using their superior speed to avoid his deadly strikes. The two foxes defended the druid, who was on his side, unmoving. Blood gushed from beneath his hands where they pressed into his throat.

No more green light. No more chanting. I watched as Yosemite's eyes shut, his face a mask of pain.

"Samir," I screamed. It was all falling apart. This wasn't how things were supposed to go.

Beside me, Alek groaned and shifted to his human form. Even in this form, he was covered in blood.

"Alek," I said. "Get back, get back."

He tried to rise but fell, his legs refusing to allow him to stand. I grabbed at his arms, trying to pull him up, to get him to the hut. I had to protect him. His blue eyes widened and he tried to shove me aside, his mouth forming a warning cry.

Force slammed into my back, knocking me over Alek's body. I rolled and regained my feet, twisting to face Samir.

My evil ex strode into the grove like he owned the place. Not a hair on his head was out of order, his coat looked like it had been dry-cleaned that morning, and smile chilled my blood. Behind him, four wolves crashed out of the woods, springing at Rose and Harper where they guarded Yosemite's fallen body.

"Stop," I said, my voice weak in my ears. "This isn't about them. Fight me. Fight me."

In the corner of my vision, I watched in horror as Ezee failed his saving throw and the bear's jaws snapped on his flank. Wolverine-Levi leapt to the bear's back, clawing huge chunks of flesh, but the bear shook his twin like a wet rat and threw the coyote's much smaller body into the brambles where he hit with a sickening smack and lay still.

I threw a fireball into Samir's smirking face. No warning, no gesture, just raw fire fueled by pain, hate, and rage.

The fire cleaved around him, washing off his shields like Moses parting the bloody ocean.

Laughing madly, Samir threw another glowing stone at Harper and her mother. I lashed out with my power and knocked it away where it exploded in a blast of heat against the ancient oak. Wood chips flew like shrapnel and a wolf screamed in pain as it was caught in the deflected blast. Harper went for the wounded wolf, but its bigger companion hit her from the side, taking advantage of her single-minded focus. She howled in agony as its jaws closed down on her shoulder, ripping into her flesh.

There were too many things to fight. We were losing and my distraction wasn't helping. Inside my mind, Tess was screaming at me to go after Samir. Focus on him. If we could beat him, then we could worry about the others.

The plan. It was all I had.

Samir came at me, gossamer wire spreading with a golden glow between his fingers.

"Fuck no," I said, pushing more power into a shield around me. I had to close the distance. My legs felt like they'd gone through a meat grinder and my shoes were filling with blood, but I swallowed the agony and charged Samir.

Alek beat me to him, shifting in mid-leap as he went for the sorcerer.

The golden threads tore into Alek's head and chest as he carried them both to the ground. A wave of magic blew Alek aside as though he were a leaf on a vent and his tiger-body twisted and rolled, leaving Samir kneeling with a snarl on his face.

I reached for the node beneath me as I ran forward. Forcing myself not to look at Alek, not to think about what might be happening to my lover, I opened my body to the raw power of the ley lines.

It felt like I was trying to swallow the ocean. Power filled me, stretching my metaphysical skin until I felt like a magic sausage. A magic pressure cooker ready to explode.

I hit him full force before he'd gained his feet, slamming my body into his, locking us together with my arms as I fought a war with the node, trying to channel all the power toward one purpose. Total and utter annihilation of Samir.

We tumbled to the ground and he tried to fight me off, but I clung with every ounce of strength left in me.

Something inside broke open, like a joint popping into place. Pain faded away. My mind cleared. All at once the raging ocean of power became a spear in my hand, bent and shaped to my will, ready for use.

I opened my eyes.

We had rolled and turned, so that I could see most of the grove beyond Samir's shoulder. Harper was down in a bleeding heap, her mother standing over her, also bleeding from too many cuts and bites to count. Yosemite lay still, his hands no longer stemming the blood flowing from the wound in his throat. Even as time seemed to slow and hang around me, I watched as the bear smashed Levi to the ground, fur and flesh flying.

Then I saw Alek. He was back in human form, blood gushing from a gaping wound in his chest. Deep cuts oozed and smoked in his face. He stretched a hand toward me, trying to rise.

Samir and I were pressed body to body, heart to heart. I heard his heartbeat, felt his magic battering me. I let go of him and space opened between us as we both struggled to our knees. He was still in arms reach. His heart in arms reach.

And I hesitated.

This was my future. I had the node at my fingertips, ready to smash through Samir's chest. To drag his heart from his body and end him forever. Mind-Tess screamed inside me to act, to do it.

And then what? Watch Alek die? My friends had fallen. I had failed every single one of them. Again.

What kind of life would I lead? Was this my fate, to watch everyone I loved die over and over. To fail to protect anything at all? I would triumph, perhaps. Be safe, perhaps. But the price. Oh the price.

It was too high.

My hesitation cost me.

Samir struck, his hand growing glowing claws as he plunged it into my chest, smashing apart the remnants of my shields, and pulled my still-beating heart from my body.

Just as it had when I'd fought and killed Tess, time slowed down even more. The world went silent other than the roaring of my own heartbeat in my ears. I clung to the node magic even as Samir laughed. Clung to the magic and formed a desperate plan that was so idiotic even Tess stopped yelling inside my mind, shocked to silence.

"Stupid girl," he said, raising my heart to his lips.

I moved my lips, trying to speak, and he hesitated.

"What? Last words? Come on then." All illusion of sanity and beauty was gone from his features. His handsome face was twisted into a mocking grimace, his eyes blazing molten gold. Lucifer, indeed.

Harper had asked me what I thought would have happened if I hadn't come to Wylde. She'd pointed out that there would be a lot of dead people. Perhaps she'd been right. There were too many dead already. I was the cause, no matter what she'd said. Samir had once again taken everything I loved, had broken me completely.

I didn't want to live anymore. Not in this world, the one where even if I won, I lost. Lost too much. Too many.

It was not better to have loved and lost. The poet got that totally wrong.

It was better to love and win.

I turned the node power from a spear into a portal, reaching deep into Tess's memories, into her mother's memories. A beautiful dark-haired woman giving her life for a baby, so that her baby in turn could give her life to a stranger.

My lips moved again, and this time I managed the words.

"Control-Z, motherfucker."

The world went black. Not the black of night or when you squeeze your eyes shut, but a deep and unending darkness that stared into me with Nietzschen horror. An abyss as complete as I could ever have envisioned, glaring into what some might call my soul.

I came apart, the magic unraveling. I felt my body burning away, my essence dispersing into that darkness. There was no pain, no sense of hot or cold. Just… nothingness.

Clinging to the thought of a new future, of undoing what I had done, of saving my friends, I fought the unmaking. I held tight to the tiny kernel of hope, of belief that I could change the world, that I was strong enough to affect the entire universe.

Nothingness faded and was replaced by a presence that terrified me more. Something squeezed on whatever remained of me, pressing in on the ember of my life. Every dream I'd had—every wish, every heartache, every memory—compressed into that tiny spark.

I refused to let go. I wasn't ready to die yet. I had too much work left to do, even though my burning brain couldn't quite recall what all I was doing here.

Like a chewed up cherry pit, the universe spit me back out.

"Jade?" Yosemite's voice called to me down a long tunnel and I opened my eyes with a gasp.

I was on my knees in the grove, clutching my D20 so tightly it had left a mark in my palm. Wildly I looked around.

Gunfire burst in the distance and owl-Junebug took flight from the oak.

I hadn't gone back very far, but I was frozen for a

moment with utter joy at seeing them alive. I had done it; I had undone the terrible future.

Now to change it, to keep the reality I'd just escaped from happening again. I'd watched Steve die twice, I wasn't going to repeat that mistake. I reached for my magic and nearly passed out. Red dots swam across my vision. It was like reaching for Wolf after she had gone. Nothing responded, not even the tiniest ember of power.

"Fuck" I muttered. Then the future came flooding back to me full force and I struggled to my feet.

A shadow moved in the brambles beyond the grove.

"Iollan," I cried. "Get us out."

I didn't know how I was going to fight Samir when my magic was drained, but escaping and living another day sounded good enough. I would come up with a new plan, after we were away. After my friends were safe and whole and alive.

I hadn't fucking time-traveled just to watch them all die again. Not again. Not ever again.

A shot rang out and Junebug fell in a puff of feathers. I'd forgotten that part, my brain a mush of what was, what had been, and what might be.

Levi tried to run for her and I threw myself in his direction as Yosemite chanted.

The bear crashed through the brambles. I had no magic to stop him this time or slow his charge and he sprang at Harper and her mother.

Green light wrapped around Levi and jerked him backward. The druid was trying to hold us together, keep us close enough to transport away.

Samir. The exploding stones. That had been next, the glowing rock and the death and pain that had followed.

I twisted and threw my hands out, working on instinct and memory as the stone flew into the grove. I punched it with my fists like spiking a volleyball, knocking it away. Alek hit me from the side and we tumbled over. The stone exploded, but the tree and hut blocked the worst of it this time. Molten pain stung my leg but Iollan's chant carried on.

He hadn't been hit. I had already altered the future. Maybe we had a chance.

Green light enshrouded us and I clung to the giant tiger as hard as I clung to consciousness. Holding onto Alek was easier. My mind swam and reeled, bile rising in my throat. Ezee and Levi were

ANNIE BELLET

wrapped in green tendrils, snapping at them with their teeth but unable to break free.

"Don't fight it," I screamed, hoping my friends would understand. "Trust me. We have to go."

I watched a red form streak by us as Alek shifted to human, holding onto me with his arms, no longer fighting the druid's magic. Harper.

"Harper," I yelled.

She dodged around the bear, heading for where Junebug had fallen. She was too far, the green tendrils from the oak couldn't reach her.

"Harper!" The ground started to swallow us, the earth shaking as the sky above because a strange and lazy spiral counter-clockwise.

She slammed into some kind of magical net and was thrown down. I watched her body spin. Samir stepped out of the brambles as the giant white bear backed away from the druid's magic.

I clawed at Alek, trying to free myself. I couldn't leave Harper behind. I felt so weak, my body full of lead and sand, unresponsive. I had no magic. I had no way to help her.

My eyes met her gaze as the white bear closed his jaws on her flank.

I screamed and shoved at Alek again, and then the green light pulled us down, covering us over. We fell through a spinning vortex of green fire, heat and cold licking at my skin.

No magic. I felt it, a void where my power should have been. I couldn't protect them.

Samir would come at us again and again, hunting me, hurting me until there was no hurt left to inflict. Only then would he take my heart.

"I love you," I whispered into Alek's chest. "I love you forever."

Then I let go of him and kicked him as hard as I could, thrusting him away from me.

I heard him call my name, and then the light engulfed me and I sank into oblivion.

Harper felt the bear's teeth crush her hip. She ripped herself from his grasp, snarling and crawling away on broken limbs. Agony was a molten knife in her body and her spine gave out.

The green light had faded. Everyone was gone. Somewhere in the woods, Junebug was down, injured or dying. Or dead.

Anger smoldered inside her. They were supposed to fight.

Jade had promised they would fight. She had said she had a plan. Running was not the damned plan.

And they'd left her. Her and Junebug. To die.

Harper shifted, her human legs barely working

better than her fox ones had. The smell of old blood and death washed over her as she dragged herself backward, waiting for the white bear to end her suffering.

The bear had backed away. Instead, a tall man with dark hair and a grey wool coat walked toward her, a smile on his face that froze her blood.

"Samir," she said.

He lashed out with his hand and magic pounded into her breastbone. Her heart stuttered as renewed agony smashed through her. Harper grabbed for him, struggling to get up, throwing a wild punch and snapping with her inadequate human teeth.

He rained down blow after blow until her ribs gave out and she couldn't breathe, much less rise. Adrenaline and desperation were a strong antidote to the crushing pain, but her body was numb and refused to obey. Refused to fight.

Et tu, Brute? she thought.

Why had Jade run without fighting? It didn't make sense. Harper's mind played the scene over and over. Junebug tumbling from the sky. Jade, kneeling on the ground, yelling at the druid to get them out of there.

Why had she been kneeling? Harper's mind fixated on that moment. Jade had been standing, radiating magic strongly enough that Harper could taste it, like ozone in the air before a storm.

Then, as though time had skipped a beat, her friend had been kneeling. No magic coming off her. She'd punched that glowing rock out of the air with her fists. Not with power. Jade always used magic, so why hadn't she then?

Harper's mind spun as consciousness warred with survival instinct.

"She left you." Samir's voice intruded. "Turned tail and ran. I admit, I didn't expect that."

Harper forced her eyes open. The bastard stood over her, staring down into her face. A crease between his eyebrows gave him a quizzical expression and Harper almost believed him, believed that he was uncertain. She hadn't expected Jade to run, either. Something had happened. Something had gone wrong. She still saw Jade's face, her friend's dark eyes begging for her understanding as the druid's magic took her friends away. She'd seen the terror on that face, the horror at leaving Harper behind.

Maybe she had planned to run. Maybe she hadn't.

Harper pushed away her anger and fought the poison of betrayal. "Trust me," Jade had screamed.

Harper had to trust her. Not that it mattered. The smug evil asshole above her was a much bigger problem.

She licked her lips, blood stinging tiny cuts around her mouth as her tongue spread the wealth. Working her jaw, Harper tried to think of a really badass thing to say for her last words. Her mind was fogging, her heartbeat so slow she wasn't even sure it still worked. She was definitely dying, she thought.

So she went with the first words that came to mind.

"You go to hell," she gasped, snarling up at Samir.

"Ladies first," he replied.

Then his boot came down and Harper had nothing more to say.

If you want to be notified when Annie Bellet's next novel or collection is released, please sign up for the mailing list by going to: http://tinyurl.com/anniebellet Your email address will never be shared and you can unsubscribe at any time. Want to find more Twenty-Sided Sorceress books? Go here http://overactive.wordpress.com/twenty-sided-sorceress/ for links and more information.

Word-of-mouth and reviews are vital for any author to succeed. If you enjoyed the book, please tell your friends and consider leaving a review wherever you purchased it. Even a few lines sharing your thoughts on this story would be extremely helpful for other readers. Thank you!

Look for *Thicker Than Blood*, the exciting sixth book in *The Twenty-sided Sorceress* series.

Coming June, 2015.

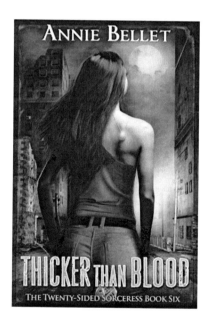

Also by Annie Bellet:

The Gryphonpike Chronicles:
Witch Hunt
Twice Drowned Dragon
A Stone's Throw
Dead of Knight
The Barrows (Omnibus Vol.1)

Chwedl Duology:
A Heart in Sun and Shadow
The Raven King

Pyrrh Considerable Crimes Division Series:
Avarice

Short Story Collections:
The Spacer's Blade and Other Stories
River Daughter and Other Stories
Deep Black Beyond
Till Human Voices Wake Us
Dusk and Shiver
Forgotten Tigers and Other Stories

About the Author:

Annie Bellet lives and writes in the Pacific NW. She is the author of the *Gryphonpike Chronicles* and the *Twenty-Sided Sorceress* series, and her short stories have appeared in over two dozen magazines and anthologies. Follow her at her website at www.anniebellet.com

CPSIA information can be obtained at www.ICGtesting.com
Printed in the USA
LVOW08s2125100416

483004LV00002B/88/P

9 781511 566223